Celesador
and the Lost Prince

JUSTIN O. POOLE

authorHOUSE®

AuthorHouse™
1663 Liberty Drive
Bloomington, IN 47403
www.authorhouse.com
Phone: 1 (800) 839-8640

Cover art illustrated by Cassidy D. Loiselle Sr.

Published by AuthorHouse   12/01/2015

ISBN: 978-1-5049-6561-3 (sc)
ISBN: 978-1-5049-6562-0 (hc)
ISBN: 978-1-5049-6560-6 (e)

Library of Congress Control Number: 2015919743

Print information available on the last page.

This book is printed on acid-free paper.

For my children Michael, Joscelyn, Alexandra,
Teremun, Kaylah, Isabella, Justin Jr.
Also in memory of my little sister Meighan
"Gabby" gone but never forgotten.

Chapter 1

On this morning, flowers fill the courtyards and line the bridged entrance. Streamers adorn the walls. The sweet smells of the cakes being baked for the celebration tonight fill the air. There will be a parade today. The peasants and people from the outlying villages beyond the court walls are beginning to line the streets and fill the still frozen River of Ice that sits behind the castle. It is a joyous time in the Kingdom of Celesador. At least for now, it is. In most cities, you would see children at play, running through the streets with laughter filling the air. But on this morn, the children are still at home instead as they each are helping prepare for a hero's welcome.

As mid-day approaches, King Mosyan, a tall man of regal stature whose bearings make it seem that he is larger than just two inches over six feet, his deep brown hair sprung in tight curls frame his lightly tanned face, with high cheek bones and a pronounced but smooth jaw line, thin sharp eyebrows arch over his clear icy blue eyes, and Queen Haylaia, standing three inches shorter than her husband but just as regal, in an elegant manner, but to his sharp features, her appearance is soft; to her husband's long sharp nose, hers is small and curved, to his pronounced jaw hers is subtle, to his dark hair her long locks are a honeyed blonde that tumble over her thin shoulders in loose waves and to his light eyes her chocolate gaze warms everyone that it lands upon, arrive at the platform set up before the frozen river to see the gathering soldiers and the parade

1

that the soldiers have walked to show the people of their return. The parade of returning heroes wound through the streets of the kingdom, through the vast courtyard around Castle Corundum and ended near the basin of the Forever Waterfalls to the still frozen river, the frozen water thick enough to hold the people.

Raising his arm gesturing to the gathered army weary from their long journey, King Mosyan proclaims to the assembled crowd, "I welcome home our family. Fathers, sons, and brothers, our soldiers who sought the quest of finding my son, Haneef, who we now know is dead. But today is not a day for mourning him. Today is about the Cleseadorians being whole again. We celebrate our warriors for the next three days and then the queen and I will begin our year of mourning on the fourth sunrise. But for now, be joyful in our family's return, go to them."

At the king's directive, Lynhavian, the second in command of the entire king's army releases the soldiers who broke from the formation in which they stood and began to seek out their families. Mothers embrace their sons and wives embrace their loves, the children hug their father's legs, as the people of the Kingdom of Celesador cheer. Carrying the king's banner is the third in command and as the other soldiers met their families, he stands and watches the platform from where the king is giving his speech, Caterrian once known as the castle orphan, now stands tall at six feet, with pride in the fact that he earned the rank he holds in the King's Guard at his still young age of twenty two years. His tall figure is slim and muscular; his hair a soft brown with soft blue eyes that still smile. His strong nose comes to a point at its tip. The apples on his cheeks dimple every time he smiles. His jaw is covered with a soft scruff of beard that of a not fully matured man.

But Queen Haylaia collapses at the end of her husband's speech. The weight of her grief too much for her to continue to stand she wilts, but before she could fall to the ground, she is caught by King Mosyan's most trusted warrior, Sandonzo, the head of the King's Guards. Standing as tall and firm as the Salahzo trees that grow in the woods around the kingdom, Sandonzo stands over all in the crowd at seven feet nine inches, he is not only tall as a Salahzo tree, but is broad and sturdy as well having been physically matured from years at battle, but his face still remains soft, his deep dark eyes matching the dark color of his skin, full eyebrows arch high above his battle wizened eyes and groomed goatee frames his chin. Mosyan rushes to Sandonzo's side and takes Haylaia from his arms.

Resting her weary head on his shoulder, he whispers to her, "My dear, you must rest. You have not slept well the past nine years since our son, Haneef vanished." Carrying Haylaia in his arms as one would a young child, down the steps at the back of the platform, the people of Celesador continue to cheer, all except one. A single figure, covered from head to foot with a hooded cloak, stands silent amongst the cheerful crowd staring where the king had just left.

Sandonzo takes a step towards Mosyan, "My king, please allow me to carry your burden."

Looking down at his wife's face, with tracks of tears still streaming down her face, he gently says, "No, my friend, she is no burden to me. I will once again carry my bride."

The guard led the grieving royals into the castle. The glare on his face alerting all of the servants that the king and queen were not to be disturbed.

Mosyan carries Haylaia through the main doors of Castle Corundum. He moves quietly and quickly through the halls, up to their chamber and through the doors Sandonzo held open for them. The King nods to his most trusted guard, signaling to his friend that he was to stay and advise him with his wife over the situation at hand.

Laying his queen on the bed, Mosyan says to them both, "Our mourning does not end today. My calling for the soldiers' return is not for me or you. I had to place the needs of our people above the perceived need of us and our prodigal son."

Grasping her husband's hand, Haylaia gently responds with tears still in her eyes, "Oh no, my king. It never occurred to me that you would ask for me to end my mourning before we were able to fully grieve together. But your decision is sound. I have missed the soldiers just as our people have. In their own way, each one is family and my suffering should not be the cause for any one of them to suffer as well." Looking to her husband's head guard, "and thank you Sandonzo for being a voice of reason whilst I was unable."

Sandonzo tucked his head down at Queen Haylaia's words. Not raising his head, he says to her, "I never would have given them before, but now I am offering to you my deepest condolences. I know that you have now entered your year of mourning and as in everything; I offer my services to you in whatever you need, "speaking to Haylaia, but turning his eyes to his friend and king. Sandonzo bows his head to his sovereigns and turns to exit the slightly opened door.

Standing just outside the cracked door, Caterrian backs up to gain the appearance of standing in wait for Sandonzo, so he would not be seen listening in to this private exchange.

Sandonzo opens the door, seeing the soldier, says, "Caterrian, we have much to discuss, I see," and closes the door firmly behind him, knowing he would be followed.

Caterrian follows behind the Grandmaster to his chamber. Once they have secured the door, Caterrian gives Sandonzo a tight embrace.

Sandonzo says to him, "Welcome home, I am pleased to see your safe return."

Stepping back from the display of emotion, Caterrian responds, "Thank you, I too am pleased to once again be home. But I must ask of you, the King, he is not self-serving as we soldiers thought during our lengthy quest," stroking his chin as he does when in thought.

Sandonzo sees the younger soldier's actions, knowing he was not yet finished speaking, waits for Caterrian to collect his thoughts. "They still hold on to hope that their son lives but have called their people home for the sake of the commoners, the peasants, and their people. We were not brought home because the King and Queen have realized their son long dead as we were told to believe, but they have returned us to our families while theirs is never again to be whole."

Sandonzo nods to his third in command and at this nod, Caterrian says with firm conviction, "There is no truer king than the king for whom we now serve. I have pledged my sword to his service years past. But I now pledge my life to our Royal Sovereigns."

Pouring each of them a glass of whiskey as the sun begins to set; Sandonzo turns to him and says, "Searching for Prince Haneef was never for the sake of King Mosyan or Queen Haylaia. He is the heir to Celesador and Castle Corundum and as much as they did not realize it, these people, the Celesadorians, our people and every tribe living on and near Mount Celese, needed to search for Prince Haneef, and now we all will grieve for the loss of not only our king's son, but for the loss of our heir as well."

Night has fallen over the Kingdom of Celesador and the curfew of the young (when the moon has reached the top of the sky, every child under the age of seventeen is to be in their homes sleeping where they can be seen by the adults of the household) has been followed by all but one household.

The peasant, Nian searches through a chest that has been hidden under the planks of the store room in the back of his cottage located in the meadow at the outskirts beyond the walls of Castle Corundum. The elder peasant tall at six feet has a weathered face, wrinkled with age and worry, his soft green eyes are wizened from age and experience, in the middle of his oval face sits a round nose that ends in a point, on either side is an apple cheek, his balding head holds thin white hair kept short. He pulls out a bundled wrapped in a heavy cloth from the bottom of a worn chest and carries it into the main room. The old man sets the bundle on to the kitchen table and he looks up at the hooded figure standing at the hearth and the fire lit there.

Nian begins speaking softly as he unwraps the bundle to uncover a sword sheathed in leather, "Our King is in need of your help," unsheathing the leion metal sword that shined luminescent as the fallen star from which it was crafted. "He has given up the search for his son, but we mustn't. There has never been a more valued person or family in either written or spoken history than that of their royal bloodline. Our king has been merciful and humble. And though they are feeling the loss of their son, you can bring them joy again; once again, making their family and the kingdom whole."

Picking up the sheath and sword, the hooded figure sheaths the shimmering sword. He dips his head at the old peasant man swinging the leion sword over his shoulder and exit Nian's cottage. As the figure mounts the all black steed, Nian says to him, "You have until the sun sets on the final eve of midsummer's festival to find the king's son and reunite him with his family and the kingdom as Celesador's heir."

The figure somberly says, "I will return far before then," before kicking his heels into the flanks of the horse and riding away from the cottage.

There was young boy sitting in a ditch prison bound by chains covering his entire body and blindfolded with a cloth saturated with filth. He was clothed in tattered and torn clothing that were sizes unfitting of his body. Lying on the floor, his thin body can be seen restless as he dreams.

In his dream, the boy sees himself as a toddler, playing in a stream with a little girl his age. Two men stand on the bank talking in low voices, never hearing their voices, or seeing their faces just always knowing that they are there watching over the children. Tinkling laughter can be heard above the babbling of the waters. The dream jumps years forward the two children are now around five and are collecting flowers in the meadow, playing tag as the same two men are walking behind them, following close to the children. Just a few years pass and the two children have gotten just a bit bigger in size now the playing tag has changed to playing with wooden swords fighting in a playful manner. In his dream, night falls and he hears a soft feminine voice singing "weary child close your eyes, as the gods light the skies, breathing slow as your dream flow to you down the stream," and just like every time before he awakens finding himself still chained in the only home he truly remembers-- the prison cell, and the chains that surround him.

Chapter 2

Mosyan dressed in a simple hunting tunic, separates himself from group that had set off with him to hunt the bear like beast that was terrorizing the lands, killing all of the saniff, a boar like beasts with two pairs of tusks that extend beyond its pointed snout one that set that point forward and the other out to either side, and ranisk, a large oxen like beast with the face similar to that of an elk, and the thick body like that of a moose, it has a large set of antlers with another set of antlers with leaves growing from the second set, growing from the first set, both sets of antlers looked as though they had been carved and smoothed, in the forests and meadows that surround the grounds of Castle Corundum. Tracking through the grounds trying to silently move through the woods, instead of finding the bear, Mosyan sees a saniff rooting in the ground at the edge of the woods.

Nian was walking through the meadow near his cottage when he saw the bear high in the trees, leaping from branch to branch as it catches sight of the something still behind the tree line of the woods. Just then, Mosyan comes out of the forest following the saniff into the meadow and that is when Nian realizes that the bear is not stalking the saniff beast, but the peasant who had just come through the trees. As the bear hunkers down to push off the branch where it is perched, Nian rushes to where Mosyan is standing watching the saniff, shouting out as the bear leaps from the trees and directly towards the man oblivious to the danger coming his way. Just as the bear hits the ground running, Nian shoves the man, ignorant of his surroundings, back into the trees and turns to ward off the bear's attack. Hands out stretched, the bear's jaws clamp down severing the smallest pinky from Nian's right hand. Mosyan blasts through the dense trees with a glowing sword in hand, mouth open in a silent battle cry. Seeing the man he had just saved coming to help fell the beast, Nian begins shouting and waving his arms, hand still bleeding to distract the bear. Mosyan slashes the bear's side, the blade going deep enough to pierce the heart and slide down the inside of the bear's torso.

Seeing the bloody hand on the man that had just saved his life, Mosyan dropped the sword to the ground. Ripping the bottom few inches from this worn tunic, he wrapped Nian's right hand to stop the bleeding. Together, they tied up the beast they had just fought and sewed him shut to keep the bear from leaving a trail of blood while he is moved.

Mosyan says to Nian, "Let me help you take this beast home. He will feed you and give you hide for clothing," offering Nian the beast in payment for saving his life.

But Nian says to him, "No, I did this not for payment. I did this as responsibility of human life."

Mosyan, taken back, bows his head to the peasant who had risked his life for the life of another, "I thank you for your courage. Because of you, I can see my family once more. But if you won't take the animal, please take this to always remember the bravery that you have and the courage you exude. Our King couldn't ask for better knights in his army." Picking up the luminescent sword the king wipes it on his torn tunic and sliding it back in the sheath before he hands it to Nian.

Whistling Mosyan calls a large black hunting steed that came darting out of the forest, Nian helps his new friend tie the bear behind the horse. Mosyan mounts the horse and rides out of the meadow and into the forest through the trees.

Just as Mosyan breaks the tree line of the forest, he is met by the group he had separated from. The largest of them is the warrior

Sandonzo from the Pautruculie tribe. The Pautruculie are a dark skinned people tall in stature, the shortest female of them measuring six feet tall, the males ranging from seven and a half to eight feet tall, naturally muscular, giving bulk to their height. But even with their bulk, and size, they are swift on their feet, almost gliding over the ground as they can run silently through most any surface.

Sandonzo, the Pautruculie warrior says to Mosyan, "My king, why did you separate from your guards?"

Laughing at his head guard, King Mosyan replied, "Ah, my friend, with all the noise that my guards make during a hunt, I would have never stopped the beast that has been plaguing our lands. But on my own, I not only slew the bear, but I have made a new friend as well." Leading the guards to follow behind the huge beast that his horse is dragging, they begin the journey back to the castle. Once they pass the gates of Castle Celesador, Mosyan call for the upholster and the butcher, telling them to work in tandem so that the bear could be mounted in his throne room in haste. "It is a reminder to me of how compassionate my peasants are for each other, that they would even risk their lives for the life of another."

Once the two men return to their homes, they each recount the events of the day to their wives. Later that year, King Mosyan took Queen Haylaia and his infant son Haneef, a copy of the king with the only difference, his hair color matching the queen's, to the meadow where he had bested the bear, so that they could meet the peasant that would have offered his life for another. But they did not go to meet Nian as the king and queen of Celesador, but garbed in peasants clothing, leaving their procession of guards at the beginning of the forest, and requiring Sandonzo to wait just inside the tree line before the meadow, to keep their royalty hidden from the peasant family. Mosyan, once again taking the persona of a peasant, introduces his wife and son to Nian. Nian, overjoyed to see his hunting companion, introduces his wife Apila, a shorter woman, with dark blond that surrounds her face, her eyes a soft light brown shine with joy, her small wide nose is soft, her cheek bones are high but soft, her lips while thin are full and plump, and nursling daughter Zahara to them.

Mosyan and Haylaia spend the day and into the dusk talking and watching the two babies play.

As they stand to leave, Mosyan says to his new friend, "Nian, we will return to your meadow as often as we can. The carefree life you have carved for your young family here past the walls of Celesador is that of a dream for any man."

The royal family goes back into the forest to meet with Sandonzo, change into their true clothing and set off to meet with the waiting guards. Over the next years, Celesador's royal family sets out for Nian's meadow as often as Mosyan's duties would allow him to leave Castle Corundum. As Prince Haneef grows into a jabbering little boy, they tell him that the castle must be a secret and he is not to tell his little companion. Each time they visited the quiet meadow with Nian, Apila and little Zahara the stress of ruling the Kingdom seemed to drain away from the King and Queen. Eating picnics, while watching the young children pick flowers, or play in the stream on the far side of the meadow; the two men always close by, knowing even in this peaceful setting, what could occur, having already fought a bear here.

Jumping forward the two young friends reach their eighth year. The two families are in the peasant's meadow. The two fathers have just finished telling the story of the bear to the children once again. When the killing of the bear is told, both youngsters jump to their feet and cheer.

Laughing at their antics, Mosyan says to them, "Go and play, for the end of our visit is coming near." And the children begin to gather their wooden swords. Their fathers playfully push them to the ground and each pick up the extra wooden swords challenging the younglings to a duel, as their wives sit by the stream, laughing at their games. Finishing out the day, laughing and playing throughout the meadow, the hidden royals embrace their peasant friends as family as they mount their horses to begin their journey home. As they leave the meadow and break through the first trees of the forest, Sandonzo can be seen watching the meadow they had just left with a soft smile on his face seeing the joy that King Mosyan and Queen Haylaia feel written on their faces while they are spending time as peasants frolicking with Nian, Apila and the children.

Sandonzo steps from behind the tree were he had been posted to keep watch, and reached up to help the young Prince from his horse. He hands the King a satchel with Mosyan and Haylaia's royal clothing gently folded inside and he tosses Prince Haneef a smaller satchel.

"Hurry now prince; let us see if you can get yourself changed before your mother and father."

King Mosyan lets out a deep chuckle and pretends to whisper to his wife, "Two against one, no way he can win." And he ushers her to a secluded area where he can assist her with her garments.

Once they have changed their clothes and Mosyan has helped Haylaia to sit upon her mare, Sandonzo says to Mosyan, "My king, I have never before questioned you, but I must know. Why have you never told Nian that he saved his king's life?'

Mosyan turns to look at his head guard and said, "Nian knows that he saved my life. He doesn't need to know he saved the king. One life should not be more important than another, no matter if of noble bloodline or not." He turned to his son who was thoughtfully watching him, picked up the little prince and tossed Haneef playfully onto his pony before mounting his own steed and they ride out to meet with the rest of the guards to begin their journey home.

Up in one of the trees near where the royal family just left sits a bird, bald with three stems sticking from the top of the head each stem folds back behind its head. His wings were long and flowing with feathers, but the wings do not fold, so they drag behind the bird. The tail feathers are six stems just as that on the head, but each stem holds a single feather. But the true odd thing about this bird are his eyes, they appear to be a solid bright blue, but as the king's procession travels past, the bird begins to blink and on the third blink, the eyes return to the black eyes that are its' norm and as the eyes fully return to normal, the bird lets free a screech and it spreads the long flowing wings and flies over the meadow away from the king and his guards.

Suddenly appears Drahre, the seer's eye. Seeing through his eyes an alluring figure with long curly hair that has shades of reds streaming though it like fire, her eye brows arch regally above her emerald green eyes, a soft nose parts her face above her thin lips of the palest pink. A soft dusting of freckles cover the pale ivory skin of her face shoulders arms and drift on to her chest. Her purple dress drapes over her slim form of toned muscles. The Queen Witch Mallari stands before him, blood still dripping from her hands. Draher says to her, eyes still unfocused, "King Mosyan has begun the journey back to Castle Corundum."

With her hair glowing like fire flowing behind her, Mallari strides to the doors of the seer's castle Chesle Peak. Each step becoming more graceful and turning into a glide as her dress begins to turn into a deep purple mist, going up with what would have been each step until she has become a head floating on an evil cloud of mist with her hair still streaming fire behind, until she reaches the great door, still secured, she turns fully to mist, dissolving through the solid wood door and out of his kingdom.

Night has fallen over castle Shade by the time Mallari reaches her sisters' castle. Lasal, Murcuri and Elixdrea are busy preparing a meal of gruel and barley, knowing their sister and Queen is coming to their Kingdom. In the kitchen, each witch is preparing some part of the meal: Lasal the gruel, Murcuri the barley and Elixdrea ladling the mead.

Lasal, the oldest, stands tall and proud, blue dress flowing around her thin frame, her blond hair shines with the many colors weaving through its soft waves. Her soft ivory skin a canvas that holds a strong nose high sharp cheek bones and a pointed chin, her soft pink lips full and appear to be waiting for a sweet kiss, but it is her eyes that hold the truth, the deep brown burn bright with a blaze that shows pure hatred, being accentuated with her sharp arched eyebrows. Murcuri stands to Lasal's right, shorter than her sister; she has the same thin figure but hers more toned showing the work she does, her golden dress flowing to a different breeze than her sisters' causing her shimmering straight black hair to flow as well. Sharing the same skin tone as her sister, her features much softer though; her nose small and ending in a soft point, much as her chin, her soft cheek bones give her apples to her cheeks making her appear to smile without raising the sides of her pale pink lips, even her eyebrows more curved give her a kinder appearance than her older sister, but just like Lasal, her hazel eyes burn with abhorrence. The youngest of the three witches stands apart from her sisters in her features. Instead of their lean bodies, Elixdrea is more curvy, a full figured woman. Sharing her sisters' skin tone, her long strong nose comes to a point; her high cheek bones point to a strong chin that ends in a soft point, her forehead gives her face a longer appearance than that of her sisters, her lips a deep red and her eyes blaze a bright blue green.

The mist of Mallari appears through the fireplace of the great hall and she metalizes back into her form, stalking down the hall as though she was approaching her prey, fingernails shaving flakes from the stone walls falling to the floor as if leaving a trial of bread crumbs in her wake.

She flicks her wrist up and the candles in the dining hall spring to life with flames, then moving her arm in a downward motion across the front of her body, the chair at the head of the table moves back of its own accord. Coming to the head of the table, Mallari brings her arm in a slow swooping motion behind her and the chair moves under her, seating herself menacingly at the great stone table and leaning back in the seat, arms draped on the arms of the throne like chair awaiting her sisters and her meal.

Laughing and talking amongst themselves the three sister witches bring the prepared meal towards the dining hall, at the door Lasal stops abruptly, causing Murcuri and Elixdrea to collide into her.

Elixdrea says to Lasal, "Why have you stopped, sister?"

Laughingly Murcuri snickers, "Maybe she sees a ghost."

Without turning towards them, Lasal whispers under her breath. "The queen, she has returned."

"That is no welcome for a queen" Mallari said in a sharp tone.

The three younger sisters rush into the dining hall and set the food upon the stone table and throw themselves to her feet begging her forgiveness for the senseless words spoken. Lifting her left arm from where it rests, she spreads her fingers and the witches begin to lift from the ground, choking as if being stretched by nooses.

seJustin O. Poole

"If we had not been born of the same womb, my dear sisters, your insolence would not be tolerated." Mallari hissed, dropping her hand and allowing the three witches to drop to their feet. "Now sit and let us speak as if we are family."

Elixdrea says in a soft whisper to Murcuri, "But I thought we are family."

Murcui hushes the youngest witch as they hurry to their seats.

Lasal asked Mallari, "Where have you been, my sister? Last eve we received your raven. We assumed it was urgent, my queen."

Elixdrea piped in eagerly, "My queen sister, we have prepared a meal for you. Let us serve it to you." And she uses her powers to place a bowl of gruel and barley in front of Mallari.

Seeing the contents of the bowl, the queen witch flicks her fingers, causing the bowl to fly across the hall and smash into the door. She jumps to her feet, swatting the air behind her and her chair flew into the wall behind her. Mallari looks to her sister's right arm extended palm upward facing and the large stone table begins to crumble. Turning her hand to the left, the table is flung across the room like a branch in a wind storm shattering against the pillar.

"This is what you would serve your queen?" screeched Mallari. "Where are the meats? Where are the finer things deserving of my status? But no, you feed me as though I was a commoner, a beggar. We, who are of royal blood, nothing less should quench your thirst." furiously proclaim Mallari. Ignoring the mess that now covers the dining hall, Mallari walks from the dining hall and finds a sitting room where she sits, knowing that her sisters would follow in her wake.

"The time is nigh." Mallari says to them as they cautiously enter the room she is occupying. "I will sneak into the king's castle while you three create mischief to distract the town's people and the guards as I slip into the prince's room and abscond with the heir of Celesador."

"Oh, mischief," Elixdrea gleefully exclaims. The sisters begin to chatter discussing what mischief they will cause that night.

Chapter 3

Coming to the edge of the peasant's meadow, the hooded figure turns the steed back from which they had come and whispers to the horse, "I go alone from here dear friend. Hurry back to the stable and my father will tend to you."

Watching the horse gallop back towards the cottage like a shadow through the night, the cloaked figure bends and fills the satchel with the berries that grow at the banks of the stream. Once it is full, the masked traveler pulls a hand carved canoe from behind the bushes and places the satchel filled with bread and berries, waterskin all but bursting with clean drinking water, a bow and arrows and the sheathed sword into the boat, pushing it into the stream that flows down the mountain.

The traveler leaps into the boat and puts the oar to water stroke after stroke taking it from the calm stream by the meadow towards the rocky river rapids that will carry the boat with great speed down the mountain side. As the boat nears the rapids, the oar is no longer needed for speed, but the traveler is using it in feeble attempts to steer the boat away from the rocks that jut out of the water, and the rocks that are barely visible in the water. Each stroke, now, is to protect the boat that was so painstakingly carved by the traveler and Nian the peasant, pushing off a rock on the right to hear the boat scrape into one on the left. The traveler continues this game of marbles, knocking from rock to rock through the length of the rapids.

At the end of the rapids, the river widened allowing the flow to slow the boat. Once again using the ore to propel the now battered hand crafted vessel, the hooded traveler was able to move the boat through the murky waters at a steady pace. Continuing through the water, the air becomes still and the trees along the banks no longer rustle. The masked traveler unexpectedly feels a tug at the paddle and struggles to keep it pushing through the now still waters. After a few strokes more, the oar once more was jerked from below the water's surface. Realizing that the foe battling the boat's paddle is hidden below the water, the figure hurriedly begins to pull it from the river to protect the hand crafted wooden blade from the unseen enemy. But before it is able to clear the side of the boat, a slender hand reaches up from beneath the waterway and yanks at the oar starting a game of tug of war as the hand continues to wrench at the paddle and the traveler refuses to relinquish it to the waters.

Getting nowhere with the oar, the hand is joined by another and a breath taking siren pulls herself up using the oar before grasping the side of the boat causing it to start rocking back and forth in the river. The siren is soon joined by another equally beautiful siren on the opposite side of the boat with others scattered on the rocks littering the river and more seen following behind the slow moving craft. Releasing the oar into the water, the masked figure picks up the bow and a silver tipped arrow, taking aim and striking the siren rocking the boat, as she is steering it to the rocks where her friends lie in the moon light. The armed traveler turns pulling a second arrow from the quiver and hits the other siren holding on to the boat, jarring the craft free from the path they had set it on and setting it crashing towards the river bank. Looking back, the figure watches the two dead sirens float down the stream, but knowing that something must be done to keep from crashing into the rocks along the river floor; the hooded figure uses the bow still in hand to pilot the boat to the bank of the river stream. Just before hitting the embankment, the traveler jumps from the boat into the cold water, pulling the boat onto the bank, but instead of solid ground the bank that meets the water is soft and muddy beneath the weight of the slight figure.

"Ugh, the Swamps of Sorrows," was muttered under the breath of the journeying peasant, looking further down the river the mountain range could be seen. Once the boat is secure out of the water, exhausted from battling both the rapids and the sirens the traveler collapses, landing face up on the soft earth being overtaken by sleep.

Sandonzo finds Caterrian's armor in front of his chamber door the following morning after the King's speech. He turns to the lone window in his room and sees Caterrian riding on top of a stark white horse heading east towards the sunrise just beyond the castle walls. Determined to find whatever news possible of the heir of Celesador, Caterrian begins his travels heading down the eastern side of the mountain, towards the Dune of the Exceltions.

Sandonzo calls together six of his exceptional soldiers telling them that their superior Caterrian has gone in search of the prince beyond the borders of Celseador. "Go now and see to it that he finds the answers that he seeks," he sends them to find him and to protect him during the journey. The six make haste to pack and prepare for the new quest on which they are sent.

Reaching the Dune of Exceltions, Caterrian tethers his weary horse to a stake in the ground near a large storm weathered door that seems to be free standing. Opening it, he steps into a pitch black corridor. Walking a few steps past the threshold, Caterrian feels that the ground is no longer beneath his feet and falls into what seems a pit.

"Umph" he lands on the dirt floor.

"Hey." exclaims a short man, who has long eyebrows that curl high towards his hairline, and curly textured hair that poofs around his head, a long pointing nose, tip sharp to a point, and he has almost fur like hair on his knuckles and on his forearms which are elongated and reaching to his knees, "Why are you dropping in scaring an Exceltion like that. There is a ladder right over there, you know."

Caterrian rebutted, "There was no sign posted instructing proper decent"

"Hmm, well, if you see a hole in the floor of where you are walking, shouldn't you look for a ladder to use for your decent?" says the Exceltion scholar.

"See," snorted Caterrian, "It is completely dark up in that hall, no one can see in dark such as that!"

"All Exceltions see through the dark, if you couldn't, you should have called down for one who can see to help you do so. Well, you are here now, just follow me, you are wasting my time with this conversation," he turns to a tunnel with some sort of luminescent stones showing in the dirt walls and walks quickly toward a large open corridor where it's many tunnels meet. Once Caterrian reaches the swift moving Exceltion, walking much slower in the darkened tunnel, the shorter man says to him, "Stay here, Eegam will want to speak with you," and the short historian disappears down a smaller tunnel.

Chapter 4

Caterrian stands waiting, looking around at the different tunnels that go in different directions from this central location. Being impatient of nature, Caterrian begins to pace the corridor. As he moves stealthily from one side to another, he begins to hear a sound echoing from a tunnel much darker than the rest with less of the lighted stones showing through the wall, receding in amount as the tunnel grew in depth. He continuing pacing away from the dark tunnel, but each time the sound draws him back. He slowly takes small steps past the entrance of the darkened tunnel following the soon deafening unhuman screams and screeches.

Turning a bend in the tunnel, Caterrian comes to a sudden stop. Just a few feet in front of him is a great beast who fills the entire tunnel. It had a rodent like body, with four stubby legs on the end of each was a paw as large as Caterrian's torso with five claws that curled in slightly, each as long as the paw itself. The eyes so sunken in that they are barely visible, a long nose almost cylinder in shape at the tip of the nose were two sets of teeth moving fast almost as a turning machine moving fast crunching something sounding like bone. On either side of the teeth is a mandible; together, they are pushing the beast's meal into its teeth. Seeing the beast spitting out dust from a small mouth under its nose, as it is crushing more bone, Caterrian draws his sword, the only piece from his armor that he kept from Celesador and rushes the beast to save the remaining Exceltions from his bone crushing teeth.

The beast turns and begins tunneling out of the tunnel, making a new tunnel as though to escape. Seeing his chance, Caterrian sinks the blade of his sword into the beast's neck drawing an ear-piercing scream from the now injured animal. The beast knocks Caterrian into the wall of the tunnel behind him with a single swipe of its cord like tail. The soldier jumps up and yanks the blade from the beast as it bucks trying to free the blade. Caterrian slices again to sink the sword once more into the animal's side as the beast turns and begins to rush towards him; teeth gnashing in his haste to end his torment.

Suddenly a group of Exceltions appear from another tunnel. The Exceltions are short in stature, the tallest among them standing no more than three inches over five feet, each one has a small button nose and eyebrows that grow long that it touches past their hair line, their age shown by the wrinkles on their face and the silver that streaks through their hair. Eegam, the Exceltion's High Scholar places his hand on the beast's head, near the wound, murmuring sarcastically, "Tundwalla, has this nasty rouge harmed you. Minding your business; doing your job and this war hungry warrior attempts to slay you. But no, my mighty tunneler, you have thwarted the mean soldier, haven't you." As he turned and glared at the offending man leaning against the tunnel wall.

Caterrian straightens himself and starts brushing the dirt and dust from his clothing, bewildered at the group administering aid to this Tundwalla beast and not the soldier who had been defending them.

"What's the matter, Rouge? Have you never seen a pet before?" Eegam questioned their uninvited guest.

"Never one of this stature." Caterrian answered inquisitively.

Eegam begins walking through a tunnel to the left of Caterrian, turns and looks at the Rouge and said, "Well, come on now, unless you want to help Tundwalla create the new library as payment for your acts" this spurs Caterrian to jump forward and follow the High Scholar.

Eegam opens a door and ushers the now weary soldier into the great hall already set with food for the guest. The room is lit with the luminescent rocks that were also in the walls of the tunnels, stacked in piles on shelves that are dug into the walls. Seeing the surprise on Caterrian's face at the meal of saniff and fresh vegetables set on the table much closer to the ground than Caterrian expected, Eegam say to him, "If you would prefer, I can set a place for you with Tundwalla and you can help him dig the tunnel and eat roots."

Hearing this, Caterrian looks to him startled and hurriedly assures him, "No, my thanks. This meal looks delicious."

"It certainly should be delicious. King Mosyan provides food to our pantry and store room." Eegam explains. "He ensures that we are fed as we keep his scholars knowledgeable on history and records. Please sit and enjoy this bountiful meal he places on our table."

"Well, I placed it on the table, High Scholar," snickers a young Exceltion, as she carries in a drink for the two men. Ushering the young scholar into the room, Eegam sits at the table in the chair facing the door and raises his arm inviting Caterrian to do the same. Caterrian sits his knees unable to fit under the table, at the setting of food as the Exceltion woman serves each of them a tonic of mulled berries.

Seeing Caterrian's discomfort at the size of the chairs and table Eegam says to him, "I would apologize for you being uncomfortable at our table, but it is not our fault that you are of the Dokeeahta tribe."

Hearing this little known fact of his history, having been raised fostered by another's tribe, Caterrian is puzzled, slinking down deeper into the small seat and begins to eat rapidly the food placed before him to divert that line of conversation.

"Now traveler, why did you decide to drop in on our people in the manner such as you did?" Eegam asked, slinging his left arm over the back of the chair in which he was seated.

Caterrian looks up from the meal he was devouring and says, "I set off from Celesador this morn before the sun had fully risen and as dusk began to cover the sky. I came upon a door standing alone in this clearing. Not knowing the language written on the doors, I attempted to skirt around them, but behind the door was a mound and then I saw the doors were being held in place with rocks, roots and dirt. I knocked on the door that read Exceltions, but no one answered. I was seeking solace through the darkest of night until sunrise so that I can start my quest anew." Taking a deep breath, he earnestly continues eating from the meal before him, not knowing from where his next meal might come once he leaves tunneled hall.

Eegam fidgets in his seat swinging his feet over the right arm of his chair, tapping his feet on the chair next to him. "Quest, a journey? Ah, so the rouge soldier is noble as well." Eegam says as he leans back over the left arm of his chair.

Pushing the large bite of saniff in his mouth to the side, Caterrian says, "I search for King Mosyan's son and heir. I will not return to Celesador without either Prince Haneef himself or proof of what happened to the young prince all those years ago."

Hearing this pledge, Eegam sits up high in his chair. Setting both hands flat on the table in front of him, he says, "I have been waiting for someone to enquire of this to me. Every ten years our young scribes come back to the dune to transcribe on the scrolls. But two scribes returned through our doors early by an entire year. The scribe from Castle of Shadows and the scribe from Castle Corundum returned saying they must transcribe the events that had occurred immediately before the spell corrupts their mind causing them to forget what they had seen."

At Castle Corundum, a shadow figure can be seen following behind the King's procession as they enter through the gates, returning from a day in the peasant Nian's meadow. Seeing the scene through the eyes of the shadow – The royal family returns to the castle hall. Queen Haylaia nods to her King husband and ushers Prince Haneef up to the castle nursery to assist his nanny in getting him cleaned for an intimate dinner between the two of them and then ready for bed. King Mosyan watches his family ascend to the family quarters before turning and leading Sandonzo to the throne room where a group of peasants were waiting him to advise them.

Caterrian, the orphan boy is hiding behind a pillar in the throne room near one of the servants' hall, hiding so that he can watch the king ruling over the people, wanting to see Sandonzo of the Pautruculie tribe who always guards the king.

The first peasant is a ship merchant, "My king, my trade's route is through the River of Ice. The winter months began much sooner this year and the ice has caused much damage to my ship. It has begun taking on water. Without this ship, I will not be able to deliver the goods I procured to the entire Kingdom of Celesador. I have used all of my reserve to patch the ship during this long winter and now have nothing left to make the needed repairs."

Mosyan looked at Sandonzo. His guard confirmed to him, "This is the only ship merchant who is willing to travel the River of Ice through the frozen months."

Hearing this, Mosyan decrees, "You will have a new ship. It is now commissioned and will be finished by a month's time before midsummer's festival."

Thinking by chance the king did not understand his problem, the merchant says again, "My liege, many thanks to you, but I have not the goods to barter for a new ship."

The king nodded his head to the man and said, "No, my fine sailor, you have not understood. This ship is being commissioned by the Kingdom of Celesador, on your behalf for the service you do for us all in bringing the items we all use, as our thanks to you for the dangerous trip you take each winter trip through the River of Ice. When none others are willing, you take up the flag of our people and sail the frozen waters."

In awe of what they heard, the group of peasants murmur in disbelief.

The next peasant to ask council of the king is a farmer, "Sovereign lord, as you know my fields provide the harvest for the castle as well as those in the kingdom who do not grow produce themselves. Last harvest, the fields did not yield as many seeds to plant and the last of the seeds have already been placed. There will not be enough seeds for crop and seedlings. There are not enough seeds to yield a harvest to feed the castle and the villages alike."

Again Mosyan looks to his guard and is given a nod that the farmer is in fact who he states he is. "Ship merchant, you did just return from your voyage. Do you have the seeds will flourish crops in our fields."

"Aye" says the ship merchant with question in his voice.

Sandonzo hands the king a purse of gems, "Give every last seed to our farmer so that our fields will be filled and our harvest bountiful."

The merchant looks at the purse astounded and sends his cabin boy out to the caravan just outside the castles kitchens and he runs back in with sacks of seeds for the farmer.

"Sovereign, why do you do so much for a lowly farmer as I?"

Mosyan replies to the man, "Your grains are what feed my people and my family. Without you, Celesador's harvest would not happen and our lands would be in famine."

The third peasant, an elderly shepherd who had spent his youth on the mountain herding the sheep that were sheared to make clothes for the people of the kingdom, stepped forward next. "King Mosyan, half of my flock has wandered off fearing the bear that is tormenting our lands. I cannot leave my remaining sheep to look for the ones who have wandered from the flock."

Sandonzo leaned down to consult with Mosyan, "He has spent his life tending to the flock that provides the wool for clothing your people. He has no wife to aid him and no children to help search."

The king sat back in his throne looking at the shepherd who has given up most of his life in service to this kingdom. He spoke to Sandonzo without looking away from the shepherd, "The three new squires attached to your guards, send them to search the mountain for the lost lambs." The king says to the shepherd, "The three squires will come to you two times a year. Each time you are set to move your herd to the new pasture, you only need to send a message to the Grandmaster," nodding his head towards Sandonzo, "and the squires will be made available to you."

The fourth peasant, a widowed mother, stepped forward to address the king. Keeping her head bowed and not raising her eyes to meet that of King Mosyan, "My king," she began in a timid voice, "my problem seems trivial compared to those you have just heard."

Mosyan says to the young woman, "Madam, no issue is too small to be brought to my attention."

"It has been a year since the passing of my husband, from a disease that we fear my youngest daughter has contracted. The healer has a tonic that will keep her healthy, but I have not enough to care for my family and barter for the medicine to keep my little Vettria alive beyond her sixth birthday which falls the week after midsummer's festival. My family does not trek the River of Ice, nor do we grow foods for the people, or even watch the sheep that gives the wool for the kingdom. We are just a humble family with nothing left to give."

Sandonzo says to the king, "This is Oleceeum's widow; he served as a King's Guard until he grew ill."

King Mosyan stands and steps down from his throne. He walks to a small table in the corner of the room pulling out a drawer. "I am glad I never did take the time to put this away." Taking an emerald necklace from the open drawer, he carries it to the widow. "Give this to the healer, this will ensure that your daughter has a supply of the medication for as long as it is needed." He turns and climbs back to sit on the throne.

Looking at the remaining peasant, the master of the horse, King Mosyan says "What have you brought to us today?"

"The stables are being plagued by the inmagus beast." This beast has the back half of a spider including the back six legs, the top half was that of a nymph with a man like torso and arms, ears that come to sharp points, its nose and mouth slightly protruding from the face, multiple layers of razor sharp teeth, and skin that is always wet with a sheen of perspiration. "We have kept fires lit at night and posted guards to keep it at bay. But every full moon, the inmagus still devours a horse."

King Mosyan looks to his head guard and Sandonzo nods to the king with a telltale smirk on his face. Knowing what that look means, he says to the master of the horse, "I will send my most trusted soldier to rid you of this beast. You will not lose any horses this full moon."

Once the peasants each thank the king, the orphan Caterrian melts into the servants' passage as Sondonzo and the king make their way to the nursery and the prince's room. Before the king enters his son's chamber, Sandonzo stands in front of the door, delaying the king's entrance. Looking at his friend, Sandonzo exhales a worried sign and the king takes the handle of the door.

Considering his head guard and friend, he says to him in earnest. "Sandonzo, you worry too much. We have left the safety of these walls of our stronghold the last time until your return. Go and defeat the menace that plagues my people. Once the inmagus is no longer a nuisance, return to us in haste."

The guard steps away from the door, closing it behind the royal family's laughter. He turns away from the door just in time to see the orphan Caterrian tuck his head behind a tapestry hanging down the hallway before the servants' stairwell. With the silence stealth of his warrior training, Sandonzo brings himself to stand in front of where the boy had hidden himself with his back tucked against the wall and his head tipped to the ceiling holding his breath in fear of being discovered eavesdropping on the king. Not hearing any footsteps or movements since the door was closed; Caterrian takes a quick breath before taking a step forward and opening his eyes as he bumps into the solid wall that is Sandonzo's stomach. Still fearing reprisal, Caterrian gasps as the fierce soldier slowly extends his hand to the boy's head. Brushing the straggly hair from the orphan's eyes and placing his hand gently on his forehead, as a father would to a son, he nods to the child. With worry on his face, Caterrian quickly embraces this Pautruculi warrior, the head of the king of Celesador's guards. A startled Sandanzo stands erect, unfamiliar with such a display of emotion. After a moment, he sets the young orphan apart from him and continues down the stairwell. The boy rushes in the opposite direction down the hall to the window, reaching it in time to see Sandonzo mounting his steed and riding towards the gates with the setting sun reflecting off of his armor as the master of the horse,

Lynhavian, the second in command and another soldier meet him near the gate and follows the soldier to the battle they are searching.

With Sandonzo riding away from the castle, cries are heard from the village. A fire broke out at King Mosyan's favorite bakery, flames leaping into the sky. With the army released from duty for the first time in nine years, the King's Guards send out the remaining knights to battle the blaze.

Chapter 5

As the sun sets over Castle Corundum, King Mosyan and Queen Haylaia settle the young Prince Haneef into his bed with a lullaby they have sung to him since birth.

"Weary child, close your eyes as the gods light the skies. Breathing slow as your dreams flow to where the waters rise."

On the last note, the king leads the queen from Haneef's room as the slumbering child shifts under his blankets. The royal parents make their way towards their chambers, the guard standing watch outside the Prince's room closing the door behind them. Turning the corner of the hall, they see a servant girl of great beauty appearing near the age of the king and queen. "Blessed eve," the queen says to the servant, startling her.

The girl replies, "Blessed eve," as she passes them, shifting into a knight of the guard. All of a sudden the king's shadow detaches and begins to follow the knight. Turning the corner the knight says in a sinister tone, "Blessed eve, indeed."

Hearing the knight coming down the hall towards the Prince's room, the guard says to him, "Shouldn't you be helping put out the fire burning the bakery?"

The knight looks the guard up and down slowly and says, "I am where I am supposed to be." Reaching out to the guard, the knight places his hand over the guard's face, squeezing his hand into a fist. With this small motion the guard disappears. Once the guard is no longer blocking the door, the knight glances up and down the hall and seeing no person, evaporates into a purple mist and floats in through the closed door. The shadows that are not seen follow the mist into the room.

Inside Prince Haneef's room, the deep purple mist fills the area above the young royal's bed as the Queen of the Kingdom of Dusk begins taking form floating above the Prince in his slumber. Queen Mallari straightens midair and glides down as if traveling down a grand set of stairs and brings herself to stand next to the sleeping Prince. Reaching her hands out in a sweeping motion over the boy she thrusts her hands down to her sides as a volt of power came from her hands and enveloped first the boy before touching everything in the room. At that moment two corners of the boy's room shadows flicker as if attempting to blow out a candle before once again becoming completely dark. Mallari lifts her arms, her green eyes never leaving the sleeping child, as he is levitates from the bed, blankets tucking themselves around the now empty bed, and drops into the witch's outward stretched arms. The boy immediately turns to mist with her as she carries him out the window, the curtains flying out behind the wake of the mist, the ends of the curtains becoming tattered as though with age leaving nothing else disturbed. Even the bed is now made, blankets fully tucked without a sleeping child.

Upon the queen witch's exit with the prince, the two shadows take their true form, seeing each other, one says, "I am beginning to forget this day."

The other says to him, "We must make haste and transcribe this immediately in the dune before this event is wiped from our minds."

The two Exceltion scholars shifted back into shadow form and wound their way through the castle and down the mountain to a clearing at the base, coming to the doors that Caterrian will enter, but cleaner and much less worn. The shadowy forms burst through the giant wood doors shifting into their humanlike forms and calling out for the High Scholar.

"Eegam, Eegam, bring us the parchment."

A small figure appears through the hole directly in front of the great doors, "Scribes, why have you returned before your time at your posts expired?"

Rushing to the entrance of the tunnel system, the two young scribes ignore the ladder that Eegam occupied and jumped down, landing with a thud and began to run down the smallest tunnel towards the transcription room.

Eegam, collecting a handful of luminescent rocks, enters the still dark transcription room. Having not taken the time to light the room, the scribes are each hovering over a parchment scroll with their eyes closed, documenting the events that have caused their great distress.

Setting the glowing stones on the table before the young men, Eegam watches them as their quills fly over the parchment. The Exceltion scribes who watch and record only age once the ten year exodus has ended and they have recorded the events they see as they shadow the rulers of the tribes and kingdoms of surrounding lands. But as these two scribes document the events of the day, Eegam is dumfounded to see them age rapidly gaining their elderly status, their long dark eyebrows first streaking with silver before each single strand turns stark white, the curly hair streaking with silver and white leaving only a few stands of peppering black near the temples of the two men's foreheads. Their furrowed brows become more and more wrinkled and the small creases around their eyes become deep as though with great age. Never before in all of his service nor written in any of the parchments documenting history has Eegam seen or heard of such a rapid progression in the aging process before the end of the full ten years of service.

Eegam called for food and drink to be brought for the newly aged scholars. But the food sat without being touched and the drinks were pushed out of the way as the scholars continued to record the events of the past nine years. Ignoring the passing of the days until finally finished, they sat back, shoulders now stooped and slightly hunched with their now aged stature.

Looking at each other, the one who had followed Queen Mallari bowed his weary head and said morosely, "It is forgotten."

The one who followed King Mosyan held his head high and turned his eyes to the High Scholar, "But it has been recorded."

Eegam and Caterrian in the great hall: Caterrian sits at the table, empty dishes pushed forward, his elbows propped on the table, and his hands folded up towards his chin. He leans forward as though to hang onto every word as Eegam tells the story of the events of the night Prince Haneef vanished.

Eegam, still in the same position, hands flat on the table sitting straight up in his chair, eyes unfocused as if going into himself to recall the events that had occurred. Once finished, he relaxes, shifting to hang his right arm over the back of his chair, setting his left ankle on his right knee, and placing his left hang upon his left knee.

Caterrian sits back and looks at Eegam in awe at what he had just been told. "Why have you not shared this with our king?"

"Your king. My people have no king. But even if he was mine, I cannot share the events the Exceltion scribes record unless the topic is brought to me. But now with this knowledge, you will take your respite here and leave upon the marrow. We are the beginning of your quest, not the end."

Caterrian stands and walks to the door which is opened for him by an Exceltion female, "Please, sir, I will lead you to a chamber to sleep." Nodding, Chaterrian follows the young woman down the tunnel hall.

Chapter 6

A watery fog seeps in and covers the slumbering journeyer and as the fog settles around the banks of the river traveled, the grounds under the sleeping form begins to move, slowly sinking away leaving a grave like hole surrounding the traveler. Little by little, the grave holding the sleeping figure begins to fill as dawn breaks over Mount Celeste. With just face and ears not covered by the oozing mud, the traveler awakens from the sun shining on the mask shielded face. Unable to move at first, the buried peasant works free from the thick mud grave. Shaking the wet earth from the cloak worn, the traveler looks from the river to the swamp to the mountain range and with a deep sigh, takes the weapons and satchels from the boat, covers it from sight and walks, using the bow to push through the sticky mud, heads along the river to the mountain range, staying clear of the Swamps of Sorrows and the sticky mud.

Once the foot of the mountains is reached when the sun reaches the highest point in the sky, the traveler pauses against a tree and takes a drink from the waterskin and a couple of berries before starting up the treacherously unstable face of Mount Ilouw. The roots of the trees could be seen coming above the ground, causes disruptions to the dirt so each step taken shifts the rocks around the tree roots; so the hooded figure uses the low hanging branches of the trees to pull himself up the mountain. The crest of the first mountain is reached as the sun sinks past the second mountain, the lack of stars causes the night to appear pitch black, with only a few steps before him visible. At the peak of the mountain, the weary traveler stretches tall before lying on the ground and he wraps the cloak around his journey weary body and falls into a deep sleep.

As morning once again breaks, the sun reaches the sleeping form on the top of the mountain earlier than the morning before. Looking over the back side of the mountain, the traveler sees that instead of the trees that were used to lever him up the steep mountain the day before, this side is covered in spiking rocks. The traveler takes a long rope from the satchel slung over his cloak covered back. Tying one end of the rope around his mid-section, the traveler makes a lasso on the other end; he tosses the rope down the side of the mountain until it lands with a thud. The figure then pulls on it to ensure it is secured to a rock. The still masked figure climbs down to where the rope is attached to one of the spear like rocks. The traveler unhooks it before he throws it down the mountain; over and over again, until the adventurer reaches the bottom of the first mountain. But instead of seeing a safe path before him, he sees that the valley is too dangerous to cross due to the spikes of rocks that continue from the face of the mountain to cover the entire basin of the valley.

Massive columns of rock almost as tall as the mountains that surround the valley before him shoot up through the spikes formed by the wind that tunnel through the valley. The flat topped columns have trees growing from the tops and spurting from places on the sides, like tufts of green hair on the back of a trolls head. The hooded figure took a deep breath before swinging the lasso end of the rope once more; this time it hooks a rock jutting from one of the columns. The traveler runs back up part of the mountain, and jumps, letting the rope swing until it brings the figure smashing into the protruding rock. The figure let the rope fly again and again many times until once instead of a rock, the rope catches on a tree. The hooded figure tugs the rope which appeared to hold tight. But once the added weight of his person is added, the branch snaps and the figure is left to free fall straight to the sharp rocks below. Untying the rope from his waist, the figure quickly makes a lasso and throws it to the nearest rock. Just in time, the rope catches and the hooded figure swings up, away from the rocks that would have impaled him. This rope was a lifeline for the figure; saving the lone traveler from harm, leaving the only damage done is a small tear from the cloak that was sliced as the adventurer swung up to the nearest rock jutting from the nearest column.

Reaching the last column before the next mountain, the traveler swings up to the landing amongst the trees and looks over the Valley of Death that had been crossed victoriously before turning back to the next mountain and mumbles, "Well, that looks like an easy hill to climb," regarding the second mountain that stood taller by half than what had been surmounted the day before.

The hooded figure wraps the rope that assisted in the journey returning it to his satchel, and climbs down the final column, preparing to journey up the mountain. But as the traveler reaches the base, a soft whispering whistle could be heard. Instead of climbing straight up the mountain, the hooded figure follows the base of the mountain, skirting the sharp spikes going towards the calming whistle. Each step brings the figure closer and with each step, the whistle grows louder. Glancing up the vertical wall of mountain, the only sure path to lead to the other side of the gargantuan peak, the journeyer pauses when at once, a wind breezes past, fluttering the hood of the figure's cloak. The traveler fingers the mask still covering the hidden face before he turns away from the summit and continues in the direction from where this whistling breeze is coming. When a few feet further, the wall of rock opens up and a cave becomes visible. The whistling wind, felt now more than just heard, signals an exit on the other side of this tunnel.

Deciding to try this tunnel instead of attempting to scale the side of the mountain, the figure strikes a flint stone on the side of the cave wall. The traveler aims the sparks to light a fire on a branch lying near the cave opening. With the lit torch to light the path, the hooded figure begins to travel into the depths of the tunnel. Looking back to the mouth of the cave, he sees that dusk has fallen, causing the fire light from the flickering torch to seem much brighter inside the darkened cavern as the sun finishes setting leaving shadows to dance along the stone walls. Raising the torch high to light the dark passageway, the traveler continues into the depth of the tunnel hoping to find that the shaft is easier than the mountain that was scaled earlier in the journey.

Chapter 7

Now that night has overtaken the mountains, the winds die down and quiet overtakes the shaft. The traveler walks on until suddenly a scream fills the caverns, stopping the lone traveler. Searching all around the empty tunnel, the shadowy figure did not move until the moans begin. Rushing towards the cries of agony, the traveler notices in his rush that the cave walls have gone from roughly carved to smooth walls, such as in the stone hall of a stronghold. The tunnel path abruptly splits into a fork. On the left, quiet with a noxious smell emitting from the dark; the right, the sounds of pain and discomfort are heard and felt. Not giving a single thought, the hooded figure veers to the passage on the right, hoping that his quest would soon come to an end. As he continues to follow the right path, the cries heard grow louder with each step. The traveler turns a corner, and sees a faint light coming from the end of the tunnel. He drops the torch and runs to the light.

The adventure skids to a stop at the sight of the doorway blocked by four thick metal bars. The traveler grabs two of the bars and shakes them, checking the stability of their hold. Jumping back from the gate just in time, the figure flattens against the cave wall to hide from two guards as they patrol the locked hall. Upon their passing, the masked figure once again steps to the bars and carefully inspects them, looking for a weak spot that can be penetrated. Seeing the hinge pin heads are rusted and covered with corrosion, the figure takes an arrow from the quiver and uses the sharp head to pry the first rusty pin from the hinge. Once free from its casing, the hinge pin flies up and into the lit hall. The clinking of the pin hitting the stone floor, such a soft sound, echoes through the stone cavern. Looking down the hall where the guards had just gone, the hooded figure, knowing someone would come check on the sound, begins to work the second pin free from the hinge. Carefully opening the rusted gate and placing it back against the hinges, the hooded figure picks up the pins and puts them in the pocket of his cloak. Checking the hall once more for the guard, the masked figure turns in the opposite direction and hurries in search of he who must be found.

The hooded figure creeps into the dungeon through the sewer system attached at the bottom of the castle belonging to the three sisters, after navigating a series of maze like tunnels. The hooded figure comes upon the room where the young boy is being held in chains and asks him, "What is your name" through the bars of his cell.

"My name is Neacel, I think" the boy replied, "or at least that is the name I hear in my dreams. Who are you?" He asked the hooded figure he is speaking to through the bars.

But his question fell upon deaf ears as the hooded figure continues to ask him questions. "When did you get here and do you remember where you are from?"

The boy prisoner replies "I am not allowed to speak or I will receive a punishment. Were you sent by the witches?"

The hooded figure answers, "No. I am searching for a boy who was brought here against his will. Have you heard of this boy?"

Down cast the boy slumps against his chains replies, "I do not know of this boy you seek."

The hooded figure states, "Then I have no use of you or your questions" and takes a step back to search for the next prison cell.

"Wait!" the young boy called out, as the figure begins to move away.

The hooded figure turns around and speaks "Do you know of who I am looking for"

Shaking his head, the boy sighs, "Though this is all I know. I am told I have been here my whole life. But in my dreams, this is not where I am from. I was in a meadow of flowers with a stream that flowed nearby. There is always a little girl there and two kindly men following behind us as we competed against each other in matches with sticks, fantasizing that we were a part of a King's guard."

As the chained boy speaks, the hood descends slowly revealing a thin face framed by tight dark blond curls tied at the nape of her neck. She removes the mask covering her face, her soft nose small but wide sets between her soft green eyes, her thin but full lips parted in amazement, and once she unmasks herself fully, she proclaims, "You are him, the boy I have been searching for. I will help you escape. I just have to find the keys to unlock your chains."

"I hear the keys come by twice a day. Once when the sun touches my face and again when the night breaths through the gates."

She looks through the window and sees the moon raising. Neacel says, "The time is upon us for the keys to be near. You must hide before they are here."

"They who?" inquired the now unhooded figure.

Neacel replied, "The keys that will unlock my freedom"

Raising her hood, she melts back into the darkness of the dungeon and hides awaiting their arrival behind a curtain decorated with the likeness of the Queen Witch. No sooner than the curtain fell back into place, the dungeon is filled with the sound of metal clicking together as the guard began canvasing each cell, every step bringing him closer to Neacel's prison cell. Peering from behind the curtain, the girl sees the chained prisoner settle back into his cell.

Hearing the keys passing his cell, Neacel screams out "Who is there?"

Chapter 8

Hidden behind the curtain, Zahara sees that the boy has distracted the guard. She sneaks up behind the guard and takes one of the long pins from the door she had unhinged; she uses it to put pressure on his neck, causing him to fall asleep. Placing him on the floor, she takes the keys from his side and unlocks the cell door that held the boy she was searching prisoner. Rushing inside the cell, she searches the keys for the one that will unlock the chains that hold the boy.

"Trade clothes with him, and hurry," she says to him as she unlocks the chains that hold him still, she steps back out of the cell, watching both sides of the dungeon hall.

"Now what?" Neacel responds, as he steps up behind her, securing the guard's cloak around his thin shoulders.

"Help me move him." Zahara begins dragging the sleeping guard into the cell and with Neacel's help they place him on the sleeping mat that consists of straw and mud and lay the chains that had secured Neacel all these years across his body. Facing the unconscious guard away from the cell bars, the two youths exit the cell and lock the metal door. They head in the direction the guard was walking, in the direction from which she had first come. They had almost reached the iron door of the tunnel Zahara followed into the dungeon when a centurion steps into the hall, heading straight towards them.

At that moment, the door she had removed the hinges from, came crashing to the stone floor causing the centurion to look from the door to the two youths back to the door. "Hey, what happened here?"

Zahara grabs Neacel's hand and turns him around, going back towards his prison cell. "Hurry, we cannot let him see your face".

"Stop, come back here." the evil guard thundered behind them as the two ran past the cell now holding the still sleeping guard.

When Neacel sees a staircase to the right of the dungeon hall, he points. "This way."

As the evil guard gets to the cell, the sleeping guard rolls over and it is seen that the prisoner is the one running up to the main hall. "Sound the alarm. Wake the sister witches. Sound the alarm now!"

Racing up the stone stairs, Zahara and Neacel reach the landing and come to a doorway covered with a curtain. Pulling back the woven fabric curtain, the two fleeing youths see an empty dining hall.

"We must go now before the sister witches call their queen." Zahara explains to her companion.

"Queen Mallari?" Neacel stops walking. He searches the dining hall for some clue as to who his captors were. But the great room held no answers for the confused escaping prisoner, barring the claw marks running the length of the walls.

"You didn't know. You didn't know who took you? Who kept you captive all these years?"

Dazed from what he had finally found out, "I only ever saw the guards. I never knew. I thought I had been born in that cell until you had told me that my dreams were truly memories."

"We must hurry away from here before the sisters find us."

Those words snap Neacel out of his daze and together they hurry out of the dining hall and through the corridor to the main door of the castle. They exit the Castle of Shade into the night and down the stairs that lead to the Talha Desert. Just as they thought they had escaped unbeknownst to the witches, a silver mist begins to materialize before their path.

"My dear, where do you run of to? Do you no longer appreciate our accommodations?"

Zahara looks straight towards the mist, while Neacel searches the area to find who was speaking to him.

As the three sisters materialize into their true forms, Neacel says in awe, "They are so beautiful, are you sure they are the witches?" Standing before them are three of the most beautiful woman Nacel has not only seen, but imagined.

The sisters' laughter tinkle around the two as Lasal stretches out her arms. Small bolts of electricity spark from her fingertips. Zahara slowly unsheathes her father's sword, never taking her eyes off the witches now standing before them.

"Your sword, it is glowing." Neacel says, mesmerized by the light emanating from the blade.

"My blade is sharp," scoffs Zahara, "that is all I need to know," her eyes never leaving her foes.

"You know that we will never allow you to take him from us." Murcuri sneers, taking steps closer to her freed prisoner.

"That may be true, but I will kill you before I let him stay here." Zahara sweeps the prisoner they fought over behind her with her left hand, her right hand holding fast to the self-lit sword.

"We will die before we let him go free," Lasal said allowing a ball of electricity to build in the palm of her hand.

Elixdrea drops her hands to her sides and turns to her elder sister and says, "I do not plan on dying today, sister." her laughter no longer sweet, but now menacing.

Seeing a chance, Zahara struck out with the shimmering blades and jabbing it, pierces the youngest sister's side.

"How dare you," Elixdrea screeches, grasping her bleeding side.

Lasal's ball of energy continues to grow and she nods to Murcuri, who stretches out her arms to her sides as wide as she can. Nodding back to Lasal, she claps her hands together as a gust of energy flashes over Zahara and Neacel before slamming into the castle, shattering the glass of every window. Just as the glass begins to splinter from the windows, Lasal pushes the ball of electric energy out of her left hand. With her palm outstretched, the two energies meet causing the shards of glass to turn into molten fire.

An angered Elixdrea swipes her blood covered hand towards the molten glass, summoning it to her. At her beckoning, each fiery drop builds into a creature of rock and fire, as they begin walking towards the backs of the two youths.

Zahara takes a step closer to the three sisters, knowing that the one she has freed survival relies on her defeating the witches before they think to summon their queen.

Lasal pulls energy balls into each hand and throws the first one at Zahara, who watches with calm as the ball leave the witch's hand and flies towards her. She raises the glimmering sword in front of her instinctively, using it as a shield. The shot of energy slams into the side of the blade, travels up the blade and shoots out the tip of the sword striking Murcuri just as the black haired witch claps her hands together, sending another wave of energy. This time, without being combined with her sister's power, the wave merely causes the sword wielding youth to slightly stumble.

Feeling Murcuri's injury, Elixdrea turns and watches her sister fall. She screams out in agony, "No, sister." Taking her concentration off of the fiery creatures she had summoned, she runs to her sister's side. As Elixdrea is kneeling over the downed witch, Neacel turns away from the witches towards the creatures as they continue coming towards him and his rescuer. He cuts off two of her fire creatures who were closing in on Zahara from behind her. Wielding no weapon, Neacel strikes out with his bare hands, landing punch after punch, knocking the rocks free of the molten fires until the two creatures are piles of steaming rocks at his feet.

"Lasal, our sister will not rise." Elixdrea stands and takes a step forward as though guarding her fallen sister. Sensing her army of creatures diminishing, Elixdrea raises her hand once more, commanding them, as Lasal takes her eyes from Murcuri lying lifeless on the ground. She begins again throwing the balls of lightning at the young girl who had struck her. But each time, the witch's shot was consumed by the sword and deflected to the castle behind her. Taking no heed to their home crumbling, Lasal continues to fire her balls of lightning energy at the young fighter.

Neacel sees that the creatures were growing with strength as the curly haired witch's anger grew. So he begins slowly to go around the side of the battlefield and picks up the dagger that has fallen from Murcuri's belt. Seeing that Lasal was occupied trying to get past the sword Zahara was holding, he steps over the middle sister and quietly places the dagger at the base of Elixdrea's throat. "Stop firing upon my friend or your other sister will be no more." his voice broke through the battle between the two females.

Lasal turns to him, arms still held out beside her, with balls of white lightning gripped in both of her palms. "Oh, dear prince, I told you before, we would die before allowing you to go free." Before finishing her words, she stretches both of her hands out in front of her, bringing the two balls of energy together and pushing them from her chest, sending it bolting towards the finally free Prince and her sister standing before him.

"No, Sister. Please Do Not" Elixdrea screams out, pleading to her older sister.

"Prince," The boy breaths turning slightly to his right, eyes searching for Zahara to question her. He loosens his hold on the witch. Just then, Lasal's ball of lightning slams into Elixdrea, flowing through her abdomen and grazes the young Prince's left side, pulling a deafening scream from the dying witch and a gasp from the royal youth.

Zahara hurries to the sides of the two fallen. "No," she cried out, as she falls to her knees next to the prince she had journeyed to find, only to see him open his eyes, now filled with fury.

"You lied to me," he said, shoving the witch off of him.

"I was waiting until we were gone from here to tell you all." Zahara bows her head to break the gaze of anger from the royal heir.

Lasal steps over Murcuri's body as she stalks towards the boy that she and her sisters had held hostage the past nine years. "She hadn't told you. Oh, boo hoo. It is of no consequence because you will not be leaving here today." The last witch standing brings her hands up in front of her, pulling a lightning bolt to stand on her outstretched hands, "At least, not alive!"

Zahara looks up and sees the murderous glare in the deep brown eyes of the last witch standing in their way of escape. She reaches out to grab her sword that has fallen next to her, only to find that it was not there.

"The only one of us who will die today will be you, witch." Prince Haneef stands with the luminescent sword stretching out before him. "I am Haneef, heir of Celesador and of Castle Corundum, I am the son of King Mosyan and I will take back my place by his side. Today you will pay for the evil you have done to me and to my kingdom." He rushes the witch as she releases the lightning bolt; it strikes the tip of the sword just before he impales her with the blade that emits her bolt of energy throughout her own body as she falls to her knees.

As the last of the sister witch falls, the sun begins to rise over the summit of Ilouw Mountain. For the first time in nine years, the sun shines on the sands of the Talha Desert as the clouds breaks during the first bright dawn since the Prince had been captured.

Haneef pulls the sword from his last captor and watches as her lifeless body slumps to the ground near her sisters. He turns and walks back to his childhood playmate. "You have much to explain." As he tosses the sword engraved with his father's emblem at her side.

Chapter 9

After a night of tossing and turning, Caterrian opens the door of the chamber where he had slept and follows the luminescent stones out to the main corridor where the ladder stood, leading to the dune's great doors. Caterrian found that his horse was still tethered outside the great doors, but the steed had been tended to at some point while Caterrian had been in the Exceltions tunneled halls. The horse was freshly groomed and there was a basket of grain for the steed on his journey along with four fresh horses tied to a lead behind him. Each horse had a saddle and a satchel of food carefully placed on their backs, along with blanket rolls behind each of the saddles. Understanding that Eegam had the Exceltions make these preparations for the quest on which he was embarking, he approaches his horse.

"I am thankful you were treated so royally, mighty steed. We must journey fast and hard. Now is when we must find the Celesador heir."

Caterrian mounts the great white beast and turns his horse southwest towards Queen Mallari's castle. He rides through the wooded lands keeping a keen eye on his surroundings knowing that the Picghana tribe has been warring with the Macindosa tribe. Continuing on his path, knowing that between the two opposing villages is the most direct path to the Kingdom of Dusk, the only areas that had not been searched during the nine year quest. As the sun rises to mid-morning, the rouge soldier hears the sounds of a scuffle to the right of the path on which he was traveling. Dismounting, Caterrian leaves the horses near the path before he heads in the direction of the fighting, unable to pass, not knowing if someone was in need of assistance, keeping to the core values Sandonzo placed in each of the King's Guards. With sword drawn, Caterrian sees through the trees a band of Picghana scouts being held off by one lone Macindosan man. Having no fight with either tribe, he would have turned and gone on his way had it been a fair and even battle. But seeing the odds stacked against this lone warrior, the rouge lets out a cry, flying onto the battle field, and he rushes out to aid the Macindosan man.

Without breaking from the battle, the Macindosan says to Caterrian," I give you my thanks for coming to my aid soldier."

"Well I couldn't let you be taken by such uneven odds." Caterrian said, joining the fight.

"I am Willetic, Chief of all that is." Landing a punch that sent one of the scouts into another, knocking both men to the ground.

Using the handle of his sword, Caterrian knocks another of the Picghanan scouts unconscious near the first two. Seeing them laid out and that Willetic was already fighting off two more of the scouts as the last one comes at him with a dagger all ready to strike, "Well, it appears my assistance was not needed." He knocked the dasher from the scout's hand with his sword. Knowing that the battle was lost, the scout turned and ran away.

With a deep chuckle, Willetic palms the heads of the two remaining tribesmen and crashing them together bringing the pile of Picghanan men to six as the only one who had pulled a knife had run back to his village. Wiping his hands together as if to remove the filth from them, he says, "True, but the coward who you ran off brought a blade to a cuff match. Without your assistance, I might have had my back turned to him and my wife would have been sorely upset had I not returned to her in one piece." The Macindosa chief stepped to Caterrian, arm outstretched and they clasp hands. "You have my thanks, friend. I could not know the outcome had you not come to my aid. I am in your debt." Releasing Caterrian's hand, Willetic raises an eyebrow in question, "Why is a Celesadorian's guard so far from the King and traveling alone?"

Caterrian answers the leader of the Macindosa people, "I travel not as a Celesadorian guard, but I alone am continuing to quest to find King Mosyan's heir."

"Let us go to my village. My wife, Morestru, will have a grand midday meal prepared and we can talk more of this quest."

Turning back to where he left the horses, Caterrian said to him, "Many thanks, chieftain, but my journey continues south west to the kingdom of dusk. I mustn't vary my path."

Willetic sees the five horses and begins looking around the trees surrounding the path, "Where are your companions, rogue? Surely you did not ride all five horses at one time."

Securing his sword to his horse, Caterrian chuckles, "No, this is my only companion. The Exceltion, Eegam had these other horses prepared for my journey. I know not who they are for."

Hearing this, Willetic begins to unhook the last three horses and mounts the lead horse.

"And where are you taking those horses" a confused Caterrian questions placing his hand on his blade that he had just finished securing to his horse.

"We have a quest to finish," said the mounted chief. "I am going to ensure you come out of this battle unharmed, as you did for me."

With a laugh, Caterrian responds, "Well, questing is all I know, but this time, the quest is one I have chosen." The two unlikely companions continue to banter as the road on through the forest.

Chapter 10

"Haneef" she says pleadingly.

"Prince Haneef, isn't it." the young royal snidely corrects her.

"My prince," Zahara retorts haughtily. "I promise to explain it all to you. But right now, we have to hurry away from Castle of Shade. We must be far from here before Queen Mallari arrives and sees the slain sister witches and that you have been freed."

The now humbled rescuer gathers their belongings and glances at the bleeding Prince, who was taking the weapons off of each sister. He picks up Murcuri's dagger and slides it into the belt of his borrowed garments; he takes the bow and quiver of arrows from Elixdrea's back and he walks up to Lasal, who had landed face down on the ground after she had fallen to her knees. Using the toe of the boot he had removed from his cell guard, the Prince rolls her over onto her back.

"Each one had a weapon that they never tried to use." shaking his head, he unties the scabbard holding the witches dark metal sword and attaches it to his side. "Thank you, I will put these to much better use than any of you obviously did." Haneef looks over his shoulder at the now crumbling castle before he begins walking into the desert sands that led to the mountains towering before them. "Are you coming, Zahara?"

The peasant liberator jumps to her feet and races behind Haneef. "The mountains are hazardous. We must stay together."

With his demeanor relaxing more with each step that they took further from the prison that had held him for the past nine years, Haneef quizzes his companion, "Well, my friend, I know you journeyed long to find me. Do you think you can keep up?" his eyebrow rises in question as he turns to Zahara who was watching the path before them.

"I can keep up, sire" Zahara says quickly.

"I have not yet said thank you. If not for your bravery, I would still be confined in that cell with no true memory of my home."

Zahara nods her head to him and says, "It was an honor and my duty, my lord."

The prince stops walking and places his hand on his childhood friend's arm stilling her. "I am still Haneef to you. We never held titles before; we will not start now on this trek."

Looking at Haneef, she said to him, "I never knew of your title until after your disappearance."

Suddenly the sands begin shifting beneath their feet and the two youths search the skies, fearing Queen Mallari had come upon them already. Grabbing Haneef's hand Zahara pulls him behind her as she begins racing towards the safety in the covering of trees on the mountain side, "We have to get to the mountain; we will be able to find somewhere to hide there," she urges him.

The escaping juveniles were unaware of the creature unearthing from a dune behind them until the ground begin to vibrate as the creature with a bulbous body and eight legs all covered in coarse hair let out a deafening screech. Looking back over their shoulders, Haneef gasps, "It's a Talhan spider."

"I thought they were just a myth." Zahara replies, never slowing her sprint.

They continue to race toward the safety of the Ilouw mountains as the Talhan spider raises the rest of his body from beneath the sand, bringing itself to its full height, as tall as a Salahzo tree. Each step it took sand falls from the coat of hair covering its enormous body. The gargantuan spider begins to pick up speed as it chases the fleeing youths. The creature begins to prepare itself for the meal it was chasing by clasping its claw like fangs together limbering them, each clamp sounding like a tree being uprooted and tossed to the ground.

Picking up speed now that the dams that had covered it had fallen off of it, Zahara and Haneef can feel the gasping breaths of the giant spider like gusts of wind upon their backs. Realizing that they would not reach the covering of the tree scattered mountain in time, they turn and begin to scramble up a sand dune to the right of them. Zahara, sure in her steps scampers straight to the peak while Haneef veers to the left, skirting around toward the backside of the sandy hill. As they gain elevation on the dune, the spider reaches its base. Pausing ever so briefly, it pushes off causing the entire dune to shift from the disturbance of the sand. The behemoth Talhan spider jumps to the peak just away from Zahara, causing her to stumble and lands upon her back. Looking up at the colossus arachnid, she struggles for a weapon to defend herself. Haneef hears her cry out as the spider opens his talon fangs, brandishing the sword he had taken from the witch he had assassinated; he scurried upon the back of the spider as it lowered is bulging head towards his companion. He turns away from the head of the spider, raising the dark blade; the prince slashes it down slicing the right rear leg, leaving only a stub unbalancing it sending the Talhan spider to slide down the side of the sand dune.

"Now is our chance. Get up while it is stunned. We can reach the mountain." Haneef grabs Zahara's hands and begins dragging her as they slide down the other side of the sand dune. She struggles to her feet as they reach the flat ground. They begin racing once more to the tree coverage on the flank of the mountain. Reaching the trees, Zahara leans up against one, taking a break in their journey to the pinnacle of the mountain. Looking up through the leaves of the trees, she shades her eyes with one hand to determine the position of the sun.

"We will make camp once we reach the top. There should be a lee there in which we can find shelter."

"Maybe we can find a stream to drink from also" Haneef replies, hopefully, as he spits sand from his mouth.

Zahara hands him the waterskin she carried in her satchel allowing him a moment to drink as she takes her rope from the same satchel and attaches an arrow to its end. Taking aim, she takes a deep breath and shoots the arrow and rope through the thick foliage of the trees. 'Thud' the sound of the arrow piercing a tree could be heard. She tugs the rope to ensure it was secure, "this will give us an anchor to use as we climb"

With a nod, Haneef returns the waterskin to Zahara. She then grasps the rope, hand over hand as she began the trek up the steep mountain. Haneef touches his fingers to the quiver on his back, "I could have made that shot." The prince follows Zahara up the mountain using her rope to aid him.

Both of the fugitives keep their eyes to the sky, watching the sun as it slowly descends from the highest point in the sky. Once they reach the arrow, Zahara sets it again to her bow, takes aim and shoots it off to once more anchor them for their ascension to the peak. The third time they reached the arrow; Haneef dislodges it and set the arrow to his pilfered bow and shoots the arrow. Expecting it to take flight as it did for Zahara, they both watch as it bounces from a tree just a few feet in front of them and lands back at his feet.

Zahara smirks and says to him, "Would you like some assistance?"

Picking up the prone arrow, "No, I will make the shot." Haneef once again set the arrow to his bow, pausing before drawing back the string. Taking a steadying breath, the prince breathes out the words, "Take flight" and releases the arrow. They watch as the arrow soars up the face of the mountain, striking a tree so far out that they have to struggle some steps up the steep mountain side to reach the end of the rope. Seeing that Haneef had not lost the training they learned from their fathers, they take turns securing the arrow each time it is reached until they finally get to the tree line.

Chapter 11

By this time, dusk has fully fallen and the stars, now visible without the tree coverage, light their way. They scale the now rocky wall until they did reach a lee with a ledge above it, providing them protection from any elements that might come upon them. With no blankets to lie on, they each remove the cloaks they wore and lay them out to use as a barrier from the cold stone floor.

Zahara takes the berries from her satchel and divides the fruits between them before she takes the quiver and bow from her back and begins to remove the other tools she has carried on her person since the night she left her father's meadow. Haneef follows her lead and uncovers the weapons he had taken from the witches. Once they had both finished removing their weapons, Zahara sat on her cloak, looking at the weaponry set before them. Noticing that her attention was locked on the pile, Haneef steps to it and unsheathes her sword. At once, the lee was lit with a luminescent glow. He brought his cloak and set it next to hers and they sit in the quiet night as they eat the berries she provided.

"It has been a lifetime since I have been in the presence of anyone other than the guards who walked the halls of my prison and they never wanted to speak to me. Can we talk a while before we slumber?"

Taken back by his words, Zahara nods and says, "There is much I need to tell you."

"What happened to me? How did I come to be imprisoned by the witches?" Haneef questions her.

"Truth be told, that is a part of your story that no one in the kingdom knows. What we do know is that nine years ago, the night after you had left the meadow with your family, you disappeared. The morning broke and your nurse maid went in to wake you. Your room was found empty. The only sign of a struggle were the tattered curtains that appeared as though they were of great age. Your father, the king dispatched his personal guards to search the lands for you. The army lost faith years ago. But for your parents, they continued their search until your father called them home just a week past. It was then my father gave me his sword and sent me down the rapids in search of you. Your father calls his army home for his people and my father dispatches me for our king."

"They searched for me the entire time." Haneef stated the fact as though trying to understand. "I have believed that I was alone in this world for what I thought was my entire life."

Zahara moves to where he sits staring directly at the glowing sword, grasping his hands, she says to him, "No, no, Prince Haneef, even though you were such a distance from your family and all those who love you, you were never truly alone. Did we not come to you and your memories, in your dreams?"

Turning his gaze from the sword that was providing the light to the one who risked her life in service to a selfless king, Haneef says, "Thank you, Zahara. You truly are a friend, not only to me, but to the kingdom of Celesador."

Embarrassed by his words, she attempts to rise in order to return to her cloak, but Haneef stills her by placing his hand on her arm. "It has been nine years since I have felt another, please lie here beside me."

She stands, gathers her cloak and sheaths the shining sword before lying down behind the shivering prince. She covers them with her hooded cloak and the two fell to sleep embracing each other for warmth.

While the Celesadorian youths slumber in their rocky cavern, the six soldiers that Sandonzo had sent to find and protect Caterrian continue on their journey through the forest and into the swamp lands. The six walk sturdily on solid ground by staying near the trees, knowing that the roots are all that keep the trees from sinking into the marsh. They walk on through the night entering the swamp and just as the sun begins to rise into the sky they come to the mouth of Oocala Pass. The highest ranking soldier holds up his hand and stops their progression. "Keep your eyes open, men. We don't need to be surprised by an Oocala beast." Drawing his sword as he once again begins to lead the men to the rock bridge over the spike rocks between the two mountains.

Stretching as he begins waking, Haneef feels the warmth of Zahara's slim frame still pressed against him, he turns his head to see his companion looking back at him.

"Good morning, prince."

"Good morning," He reaches towards Zahara, smiling up at him, but his hands only touch air.

Startled from his dream, Haneef sits up on the makeshift bed, searching the lee and noticing that her cloak and weapons were missing from the pile. He gets up and begins gathering his purloined weapons. Throwing his cloak around his shoulders the prodigal prince sets out in search of his misplaced rescuer.

Zahara stands on the peak of the Ilouw mountains, looking down at the bridge they would use to cross the valley to the second mountain. She hears Haneef crest the mountain, "Good morning, prince."

Haneef smiles, remembering the dream that had brought him awake, shaking his head as though to clear it, "Zahara," He says, attempting to tell her of the sound as though someone was climbing the mountain behind them.

"This is where we will cross." she interrupts him.

"Zahara," he tries again to warn her.

"Did you bring everything? The sooner we start, the faster we can cross."

Haneef, ignoring her words, looks down the face of the mountain they had scaled the night before, seeing a creature as it broke the tree line onto the rocks below.

"Zahara, we have to go now. A beast is coming," his frantic tone finally catches her attention. He points down the mountain side that they had traveled as two more beasts break through the tree line.

The beasts, almost human like in body with arms that reach down almost to their back knees when standing on their hind legs; hunched at the shoulders due to the bulk of muscle in their shoulder and back; the hind legs shorter in stature show the strength of muscle as well. Their skin always shines with the sheen of perspiration. Each beast has a long sloping forehead with the hair line beginning at the top of the head, showing the thinning, yet thick strands of hair. Their piercing lime green eyes sunken into their skulls; their noses are two slits on either side of the bone creating a slight bump in the middle of their face. Their ears are large, coming to a sharp point. Some have taken spike rocks from the valley between the mountains and pierced their lower lobes. They each have fangs that protrude from their bottom gums pushing their bottom lips out reaching up to their noses, with squared chins giving bulk to the high protruding cheekbones. Covering their massive forms are animal hide tunics and pants. The tops of their bare feet and wide toes show patches of bristly hair. The same patches cover their upper arms and some forearms, as well as some of the creatures' chests.

"Oocala beast. Yes, we go now." she picks up her bow and quiver from a boulder next to her.

No longer traveling with playful banter they used to motivate them up the mountain, the two begin to hastily descend from the summit rushing to the rock bridge below.

"The beasts are gaining on us." Haneef gasps between breaths, looking over his shoulder, stumbling over a rock.

"Keep your eyes on where you are going. Looking back takes away time and attention from the end goal." Zahara quotes her father.

Haneef's body stiffens while he continues running away from the Oocala. But in his mind, he goes back in time as he hears those words in his memories softly spoken by an older man; in his mind, he sees a little girl fly past him, whooping as she crosses a finish line.

"Oocala Pass, we have almost reached it." Zahara hefts her quiver back into place on her back, as she slides a few feet when she steps on a loose rock.

Haneef keeps his eyes forward even though he longs to turn and see what is causing the rocks to move on either side of them. "Zahara, something more is coming."

Glancing to the right and left, Zahara sees that they are no longer being chased by three Oocala beasts. But now swarming towards them from every side of the mountain, the mountain was covered with the beasts like swarming insects. Just as the two youths hit the ledge before the bridge, the rocks behind them began sliding down around them.

Zahara screams out "We have to cross the pillars before the rock slide over takes us."

Haneef looks past the towering square pillars that meet as an x; having fallen together after years of rock slides caused by the Oocala running up and down the faces of the mountain, and sees six figures running across the expansive stone pass. "Zahara, do you see them?" Haneef points to the men heading to them with swords drawn.

Zahara takes her eyes from the Oocala chasing them to the soldiers rushing to their aid. Allowing a sigh of relief to exhale when she sees the same emblem on their tunics as the one emblazoned on her sword.

"Hurry across;" shouts the soldier, leading the guards, "They are closing in on you."

Finally reaching the portal of the bridge and running under the crossed pillars, the two, tired from their trek, get a burst of speed as they get closer to the soldiers.

"Go on across. We will hold the beasts back." The soldier says, as they reach the young Celesadorian travelers.

As the two keep running the length of the bridge, they hear scratching on the underside of the stone walk on which they are traveling. They do not slow their pace, looking back only when they hear the first of the soldiers strike a beast down running on towards the Swamps of Sorrows.

Behind them, near the other side of the bridge, the six soldiers keep fighting the Oocala, who are now making clicking sounds as they battle, and are now swarming the bridge the soldiers are determined to defend. Five of the six guards are swatting the creatures down, using their swords. While one stands in the middle of their circle using his bow and arrows. Each of his arrows strike a target, leaving dead Oocala littering the mountain while the Oocala that fall by the swordsmen pile before the circle of men. The soldier archer, once his quiver has been depleted, begins taking arrows from the backs of his companions as they continue to fight off the Oocala that they scale the mountain of slain before them, until finally the last arrow is released. Suddenly it is quiet as the Oocala stop clicking and a beast taller than most of the others rushes up the pile from the ledge of the taller mountain. Reaching the top of his fallen brothers, it raises both arms across his broad chest and snatches the large spike rocks from his ears; right hand to left ear and left hand to right ear. With a war cry that roars echoing through the valley, he uses his powerful legs and pounces onto the leader of the king's guard. Each of the remaining Oocala let out a war cry of their own and they finally overtake the soldiers.

Having finally reached the Swamps of Sorrows, Haneef and Zahara turn back and look to where the soldiers have been fighting, but instead see the Oocala leader standing atop the pile of fallen holding one of the soldiers by his tunic that bears the emblem of King Mosyan.

"Tell your king that Queen Mallari's wrath has been brought down upon his kingdom." The beast snarls to the soldier, holding him over the edge of the bridge. Turning his head to look at the prince, his sunken lime green eyes never leave the prince's gaze; he releases his hold on the soldier. "You know what, never mind." The soldier's anguished screams echoes through the valley until they dissipate as he dropped into the dust and fog below.

The Oocala breaks the prince's gaze and looks to where the soldier had fallen. With his gaze finally free from the horror he had witnessed, Haneef turns to see Zahara running into the swamps and he begins to follow her into the wetlands.

A piercing scream of tormented grief slices over the mountain, the tortured cry fills the valley and seeps into the swamp. The Oocala stop celebrating and look to their leader, who at the sound, hunches down as if ducking from an aerial attack. Once the echoes of the cry fade, the Oocala straightens to his full height and points over the mountain and begins clicking in urgency.

As the heartbroken cry is heard in the swamps, the bats in the trees and all of the creepy crawling creatures emerge from their hiding places, emitting a shrill of their own. The abrupt movement of every creature causes the grounds beneath Haneef and Zahara to shake. The displacement shows the instability of the swampland. Haneef stops, waiting for the shaking to cease.

Seeing this, Zahara says to him, "We cannot stop yet. Mallari has discovered her sisters." She pulls him further into the swamps and away from the rocky hill. The deeper into the swamp the muddier the path and the trees begin to appear different. Instead of the branches reaching to the skies as the ones on the mountains, the swamp trees branches curve down as though weighted. Some branches create tunnels that can be walked under. The bushes and brush are so high amongst the trees that the tree tunnels are the only way to navigate through this part of the Swamp of Sorrows. The two walk on through the dense trees, unable to see the position of the sun until they finally came to the end of a tunnel that was made up of miles of trees and mud filled paths.

The first clearing they came upon, Zahara stills Haneef with a soft touch on his arm as he almost walks past her. "We will make camp here." Looking up to see the sky finally visible, and seeing complete darkness, he stops and turns to her. "I did not realize that night had fallen." He begins gathering twigs and any dry brush he can find, as she lay out her cloak and disarms herself. Returning to the clearing with the kindling, Haneef lights a fire, sets down his weapons and removes his cloak. Standing before the fire warming his hands, he hears Zahara pulling something from her satchel. Sensing her behind him, Haneef turns to her outstretched hand and takes the piece of bread she offers to him.

Together the two sit on her cloak, devouring the last of her food supply. Finishing his portion first, he turns and watches her for a moment before speaking. "They took my memories from me, Zahara." Turning back to face the fire as she finishes her dinner, he continues, "but even though I didn't remember my life, my family or you, I always missed you."

Pulling him down to lie next to her, Zahara says to him, "There was not a day that passed which you were not missed by your parents, your kingdom and me." She turns from her back onto her side to face him, waiting for his response. When he doesn't respond, she leans close, shutting her eye. Once she is near enough to kiss him, he snores loud and long. Opening her eyes, she looks down at his sleeping form and brushes the hair from his forehead. Leaning the rest of the distance, she places a kiss where the hair had just lain. She lies down next to him rolling onto her other side, facing away from the sleeping Prince; she slides her foot behind her and kicks his left knee.

The kick startles Haneef from his slumber, "I'm awake." The prince sits up, and sees Zahara curled on her side appearing to be slumbering. He glances around the camp before lying back down and pulling her close to him and once more falls to sleep. Content Zahara smiles and sighs, feeling safe in his arms; she allows sleep to overtake her.

Queen Mallari sits still on the ground surrounded by the bodies of her sisters when the Oocala beast leader reaches the castle grounds.

"My queen, I heard your cry."

Looking up to the creature, Mallari says to him "I command every beast, witch, warlock and inhabitant of the kingdom of dusk to convene for the council of war." At the end of stating her decree, the witch queen tears her raven tattoo from her left breast, leaving on her chest an arrow that had been in one talon and a venomous snake that had been clutched in the other talon. She throws the dark bird into the ink black sky it takes flight, as feathers that fall with every flap of its wings turn into another bird until the skies fill with ravens flying to every corner of her kingdom.

Chapter 12

Waking from the damp chill in the air of the Swamp of Sorrows, Haneef feels before he sees that the fire had burned down to mere embers. He pulls his cloak over his sleeping companion as he slides himself off the cloak they slept upon and walks away from their camp to relieve himself going just far enough to ensure privacy. Once finished, Haneef turns back in the direction of the camp and where Zahara lies sleeping. But to the right, through another tunnel of trees, he sees what he thinks is his mother floating before him.

"Come to me, son. I have missed you so." a soft voice from his dreams beckons him. Each step the prince took towards this ghostly mother did not bring him any closer to her. She remained just out of his reach.

Back at the camp, Zahara is startled from her sleep and reaches out for the safety of Haneef, but her search comes up as empty as the spot where he had been lying. Feeling the spot was rapidly cooling, Zahara realizes that the prince was not still at camp and she jumps up, collecting both her and his weapons and cloaks, fastening hers as she moves swiftly into the depth of the swamp.

"Haneef," She calls out, seeing a figure on the path before her through the fog. But the stupefied prince hears nothing but the soft voice of his dreams. The deeper they travel into the swamp, the denser the fog around swirled about them. Zahara never takes her eyes off the mesmerized prince being led to the murky waters by the weeds that beckon him. But to his eyes, he was reaching for his mother's hands.

The branches of the twisted trees begin to rustle. Zahara sees vines weaving their way out of the tree tops, winding down to further urge the prince deeper in the swampy marsh as if a soft touch to his back was encouraging his journey.

"Come son, we are almost home." the rustling trees spoke to the prince as his mother floated before him; still now floating on top of the water before him.

"Wait mother, I am coming." Haneef calls out to the apparition as he begins walking out into the swamp waters.

"Haneef" Zahara yells out to him, trying to gain his attention away from the being that was drawing him into the lake. She plunges into the water behind him. The leaves curling around her legs under the water hold her back as other weeds push Haneef waist deep, then shoulder deep until Zahara could barely see his head bobbing above the water with every step he takes.

Pulling Haneef's dagger from the bundle of weapons she carries, Zahara begins cutting the weeds away from her tangled legs.

"Stop Haneef, do not be fooled." She screams as she sees his head dip below the turbid drink. But his mind was overtaken with his desire to be reunited with his mother.

On the far side of the swamp's lake, two figures cease leaping from root to root as they see someone struggling in the water. They race around the bank to where they could be close to the two that have gone under.

"How many are in the water?" Caterrian asks his companion as they near the spot where Zahara can be seen fighting with the weeds.

"I spot two places where the water is disturbed" Willetic answers, eyes never leaving the surging waters, keeping track best he can of those now drowning in the murky water. He thrusts the hide cape from his shoulders and drops his satchel as he leaps on to a low hanging tree branch. Sword drawn, he dives into the lake close to where he saw the final moments in the deepest parts of the water.

Knowing Willetic would find the submerged captive, Caterrian continues to the other figure still battling the weeds that are holding her under. He reaches the bank closest to her and carefully removes his cloak. Tying it to a vine, he wraps the end of his cloak around his left hand giving him anchor as he steps onto a rock protruding out of the inky waters. Carefully watching the water, he stretches out his right arm just as Zahara's left hand emerges, still swiping at the weeds with the dagger in her right hand.

Slicing through the water with every stroke; Willetic's blade cuts through the weeds that are trying to grab him. He sees the young man being held underwater by the weeds that had deceived him. Willetic reaches the young boy and cuts Haneef free from his bond and pulls the unconscious body with him as he propels through the murky water, dodging the weed seeking limbs on which to hold.

Caterrian grasps the flailing arm; grabbing her wrist. As he begins to pull her from the water, she clutches the lifeline given to her. Water cascades over her face and down her hair, as she rises from the water like Venus, as Caterrian liberates her from the weeds holding her captive. The impact of the weeds releasing her causes her to collapse onto her rescuer, both toppling to the ground. Caterrian makes sure to shield her from the impact of the ground itself.

Zahara gasps for life giving breath and opens her eyes to see Caterrian smiling up at her.

"It's a good night for a swim. Too bad I couldn't join you."

Willetic continues to kick and fight his way to the surface, not realizing the floor of the lake was moving because something was disturbed by their struggles. Breaking the surface of the water, Willetic drags the comatose youth to the bank and sees his companion Caterrian with his arms still around the one that he had saved.

"Hmm, Caterrian, I do hate to dislodge you from your current position, but I think the young man could use your touch of healing."

Zahara, hearing another voice, pushes away from her rescuer. Caterrian is unable to scramble off of her due to his continued hold on her.

"Healing sir, remove your hands from my person. I must aid him."
She says finally dislodging herself from his hold. Zahara scurries to
Haneef on hands and knees, while Caterrian stands and strides to
the prone form lying lifeless on the beach. The rogue slams his fisted
hand on Haneef's chest. At once the boy sits ups, spitting water from
his mouth and opens his eyes.

But Haneef did not once glance at the three who had rescued him
but his eyes stay glued on the lake behind them. "Zahara, my sword,
give me my sword!"

Thinking that he was speaking of the two strangers before him,
she reaches out to him saying, "They came to our rescue. We have
nothing to fear from them."

But while she spoke, Willetic heard the water's movement and
turns slowly to the lake, drawing his sword as a two headed serpent
appears from the depths of the water.

Caterrian senses the change in the air around Willetic and draws
his sword as he turns to the lake. "It is a petilo." At his words, the
beast slithers over the surface of the water using the weeds to keep it
above the surface, coming straight toward the four who had disturbed
his slumber.

"His fangs are deadly sharp. But beware of the venom that is
released from the strike of its tail." Willetic warns the three other
standing beside him, all with swords in hand.

The petilo surges from the water to where they stand; one head
snapping at Caterrian, the other head slamming into Willetic as if
an attempt to knock him down but both stand their ground sparring
with the fangs of the beast.

Haneef, seeing the heads are distracted, runs behind the snake.
"Zahara, we will cut it off from behind."

"Wait, boy, the tail," Caterrian calls out, spurring Zahara to
follow the prince.

Haneef, not hearing the warnings, jumps onto the Serpent's back
and begins to attempt to strike the place where the necks split, but
the scales were like armor and deflected every plunge of his blade.

Caterrian and Willetic keep battling the petilo's heads, ducking away from the sharp fangs, reeling back and forth, distracting the beast from the young boy's foolish attack. Zahara scales the snake's armor plated skin to join Haneef in his assault on the creature.

"If we can pierce the reptile's lamella, we can cut off the heads," Haneef explains his plan of attack to Zahara, as he continues to hack in vain at the neck of the slithering beast.

"Water nymph, do not forget the strike of the tail. Its venom is deadly." Caterrian calls out to Zahara, as he once more ducks under Willetic's sword to stay out of reach of the hinged jaw of the petilo.

Under his breath, Willetic teases the rouge soldier, "Nicknames already, huh?"

Haneef, paying no mind to Caterrian's renewed warning, persist in his attempts to battle the thick skin, never once looking to the tail that already has poison beginning to drip from the sharp point. But Zahara did see; striking the neck of the snake and turning to see the venom soaked spear of a tail beginning its descent in Haneef's direction. Knowing that the strike was imminent, she runs across the expansive back of the petilo as the tail continues its downward strike in search of whomever it is that is pestering its neck. She reaches the prince, just at the tail finishes the descent, and pushes him off of the snake's back as its tail misses him, but instead slices through the left arm of her tunic, scratching the skin of her bicep as she falls off behind Haneef.

Caterrian sees the creature's tail strike her as he lands the final blow with the handle of his sword to the side of the snake's head that he was fighting and runs over to the downed pair. Grabbing Zahara's injured arm at the elbow, he yanks her to her feet, and calls out to his companion who is still battling the two headed snake.

"Willetic, allow us a safe retreat."

"I will give you one chance." Willetic says, beginning a backwards dance away from the others.

"Ready when you are." Caterrian begins pulling Zahara away from the snake by the hand that he now holds.

Once the three had gotten a few steps away from striking range of the tail, Willetic turns the dance into a run and then with the agility of a cat, he jumps from the ground to a low hanging branch and leaps from the branch to a vine quickly climbing to the treetop, with the snake quickly slithering after him. Twisting and tangling through the many vines hanging from each branch Willetic, still holding on to a vine, dives down wrapping the snake's necks with the vine entwining him to the tree trunk. Once the snake was secure against the tree, Willetic releases the vine, finishing his dive to the ground by tucking into a role as he hits the ground. Then in one smooth movement, he rises, still in motion, running after Caterrian, Zahara and Haneef.

Before long, his strong strides overtake the three fleeing the wrath of the petilo. Passing them, he quips, "Better keep up. I'm not sure how long that will hold him."

A loud cracking is heard through the swamp and then the ground shook as a thud sounds; a tree being broken and landing, parting the water of the swamp, sending the snake back to the depth of its watery cavern.

Chapter 13

The four companions continue their race out of the swamp that almost claimed them, not stopping to rest until they exit of the Swamp of Sorrows and enter the forgotten forest where the trees and brush are covered in thorns thick with sharp like daggers covering the tree trunks. From the tip of each thorn, a black flower sprouts. The center was a deep purple; the end of each black pedal where it connects to the stem, an almost luminescent blue brings the illusion that the flowers glow. Every time one of flower is brushed against, its pollen is set free in the air, releasing a toxin. But the travelers did not know that the forgotten forest was under the spell of the Warlocks of Veldazklek and that the beautiful black lotus flowers were added by the warlocks to warn them of intruders entering and exiting Queen Mallari's lands. The toxins are just for fun as they altar the mindset of all who inhale it or touched by it on their skin.

Zahara, weakening from the venom of the petilo's tail is the first to succumb to the warlock's poisonous pollen.

"I didn't need you to pull me around like a disobedient child." She chides Caterrian, yanking her hand from his grasp.

A startled Caterrian stumbles backwards into a thorn covered tree trunk and becomes covered in the pollen. As it settles on his cloak, he tries wiping it from him. The pollen sticks to his hands before seeping beyond his skin.

"Well," Caterrian snidely retorts, "if you weren't acting like such a blasted gnashgab, I wouldn't have had to pull your weight behind me. Neither my companion," swinging his right hand towards Willetic, "nor yours" pointing to Haneef, "needed any encouragement in our escape."

Between him bumping into the tree behind him and swinging his arms around in the direction of the companions he mentioned, the air was thick with the poisonous pollen.

Haneef takes a deep breath, the pollen tickling his nose causing an eruption of sneezes between which he scolds Caterrian, "You, sir, did not give her a chance to find her feet before you begin pulling her behind you."

Willetic snorts, "So much for getting a 'thank you' for saving our hides."

"I did not expect a 'thank you' from these children." Caterrian turns from the group and starts once more to trek through the unruly forest.

"Them? I meant you. Was it not I who tied the beast to a tree while each of you ran for the cover of these trees." shaking his head, as he takes the path following behind Caterrian.

Zahara turns to Haneef as Caterrian and Willetic can be seen walking away from them, "I do not need you to save me, you know. I am the one who has rescued you." She places the tip of her bow to his back and prods him to follow the strangers who had fought to save them just earlier that night

"Why would I continue allowing you to lead me? You keep bringing me to creatures I must defeat." Haneef begins to mutter under his breath.

"Defeat? You have not done much more than agitate the creatures and run away from them." Zahara mutters back.

Caterrian, now leading their procession through the mystical forest, rolls his eyes while listening to the childhood friends bicker. "Can't you to stop fighting? You argue like siblings over the last bowl of custard. Stop bickering, so we can get out of this forest."

As dawn begins to break, the warlock's cursed flowers travel back inside the thorns taking with them the toxic pollen that keeps the travelers agitated with each step they take their addled minds begin clearing.

"This inept buffoon is not my brother. I was sent by my father to find him." Zahara spat.

"Her? A peasant? My sister?" Haneef lets out a uproarious laugh.

Willetic places a hand on Caterrian's shoulder, "Caterrian, who is it that you seek?"

"It cannot be him." Caterrian shakes his head as to clear the fog from his mind.

Zahara and Haneef keep squabbling as they walk on past their guides.

"Prince Haneef." Caterrian called out to the young man who was walking out of the Forgotten Forest with his female companion.

Haneef looks back over his shoulder, blonde curls showing through the dirt and filth coating it and ice blue eyes blazing from befuddlement caused by the toxins he had inhaled. "What?" both the royal heir and Zahara, his peasant friend, stilling when they see Willetic and Caterrian have stopped walking.

Willetic and Caterrian, seeing the Royal heir clearly for the first time, drop to a knee, bowing their heads, swords unsheathed before them.

"I have been searching to the ends of the kingdom for you for the past nine years." Caterrian says reverently, never lifting his head. "Your father has never lost hope that you would be found." He raises his eyes to the one he was questing.

Willetic keeps his head bowed, but says to the Prince, "I am honored to pledge my sword to you,"

Haneef, confused by the display before him, look to Zahara, "even though I was born royal, such a display is new to me." He takes a few steps to stand before the two men still bowed before him. Haneef draws the sword and kneels before them, "Just as you have pledged yourself to my service, I pledge myself to each of you, for you are our saviors."

Hearing the heir of Celesador humbling himself before them, the two rogue fighters lift themselves to their full height and the prince does the same. The three reach out and clasp hands together. A disgusted Zahara sighs, "Boys, not one of you is worth the silk of my garments." She turns and walks out of the dense Forgotten Forest and into the woods surrounding the far reaches of the kingdom of Celesador.

The three males burst with laughter at her sarcastic remark. But Haneef, still concerned over his childhood playmates behavior, asks, "What do you think is wrong with her?"

While Caterrian and Haneef look after Zahara, Willetic, head now clear, notices the flowers returning to the thorns and plucks one before it fully disappears. "A black lotus; these buds are the work of the Warlocks of Veldazklek. They are bewitched. See the purple dust, it corrupts your mind. This is why we argued through the entire forest."

Caterrian looks closer at the flower shriveling in Willetic's hand. "If the warlocks have bewitched them, then they know where we are. We must hurry from the here before they come find us."

"The shock we received discovering the truth of who you truly are was enough to wake our minds from their daze. But we know that her mind is still disturbed." Willetic is thoughtful in his response as they walk past the very last of the hexed thorn flowers.

"I must break the spell." The valiant prince said, picking up to speed to reach the seemingly confused Zahara.

Caterrian chuckles at Haneef's words. "We are free from the toxic air. She will clear soon." But his words fell on deaf ears as Haneef has already reached her side.

Willetic touches Caterrian's arm and says, "Leave the boy; he's doing what he feels right."

"Zahara, you need not be distressed." Haneef says to her, "it was the pollen that has affected your mind. This is why we quarreled through the dense trees."

"Haneef, my mind is clear. But how is it that you bond so quickly with these two rouges, going as far as the pledging swords to each other. Wasn't that my blade that helped free you from your foul prison cell? You clasped hands with these strangers. Well, I assisted in your escape from the castle and the Talhan spider." His despondent friend explained.

Gazing into her green eyes, Haneef brushes the strands of hair away from her face and behind her ear. "Zahara, I could never forget what all you have done for me. Without you, I would not be free from my captors." He takes her hand in his, "memories turned into dreams of you are what kept me sane during the years I was in prison. I have not forgotten how I pledge my service to you when we played with wooden swords. Even before I remembered your name, you never did leave my heart."

Zahara's eyes, glistening with unshed tears said to him, "I pledged my sword to you when we were still children. But now I pledge my friendship. Before, I did not understand what that meant. But now I do."

Caterrian and Willetic join the two. Caterrian smacks Haneef's shoulder, jarring Haneef and Zahara from the moment they were sharing. "Who else is famished? Shall we break our journey for lunch?" He turns from the group and sits on a rock. Willetic follows his lead and joined him, sitting on the ground near him. Both takes bread from the satchels they carry.

Walking to where the two rouges sit, Zahara removes the water skin from her bag, taking a drink before handing it to Haneef.

Sharing a look with Willetic, Caterrian takes the last piece of bread from his own satchel and hands it to Zahara, who breaks it in two, before passing the larger piece to the prince.

Willetic, having finished his lunch reclines back on his arm before asking, "Zahara how did you cross paths with the prince?"

Bristling from the comment, Zahara looks up at the two rogue soldiers through hooded eyes, "We crossed paths when I broke into the prison where he was being held and went to gain his freedom. Where have you been the past week or so?" She tosses her hair over her shoulder.

Willetic begins to laugh at her comment, "she has us there Caterrian, while you were on a leisurely ride, this imp has finished your quest." He slaps the rouge's knee.

Haneef tells the story of the battle that he and Zahara fought against the sister witches. Going into detail about the witchcraft that was used against them and how Zahara deflected it from even hurting them. "Well except for this" the prince lifts his tunic to show the burn that was left on his side.

Caterrian looks at this peasant warrior who has, and is risking her life for the prince, and the kingdom. "Deflecting the witchcraft?" He questions her.

"I don't know how, but my sword became as a shield, it protected us from them." She tells them, "But the prince was the one who finished the battle." This time she deflects the questioning eyes trying to probe her.

"How so?" Willetic asks, giving a brief nod to her with a slight smile.

This simple question broke Haneef into the tale of how he defeated Lasal, and how he found out who he truly was. After telling their new companions about their escape from Castle of Shade, the prince excitedly tells of their journey through the Talha Desert and how they battled the giant Talhan spider. Zahara watches with a peaceful smile on her face the price in his excitement telling of the climb up the Ilouw Mountain and going into the story about the Oocala beasts.

But when he says that six soldiers saved them at the Oocala Pass, Caterrian stops Haneef's recount. "Soldiers, whose colors did they wear?" He directs his questioning gaze to Zahara.

"They were King Mosyan's guards," she told the rouge guard quietly.

Haneef becomes sullen, remembering the actions of the leader of the Oocala beasts, and of the soldiers who fought to protect them, never asking who they were or even where they were from before coming to their aid.

The four travelers sit quietly thinking over the journeys that have brought them all together.

Willetic stands and stretches, "We need to continue on our way."

Caterrian stands as well, and says, "My horses should be just beyond the trees."

"Horses," Haneef says with a soft smile as he begins to walk in the direction Caterrian had pointed. The others look at each other and laugh at the joy in the prince's voice before falling in behind him.

Willetic and Caterrian being wiser from age walk the group along the forgotten forest's edge staying just far enough away from the warlock's toxins to ensure they aren't afflicted by the pollen, bantering to each other as they search for Caterrian's hidden horses.

As they come upon the hidden glen where Willetic and Caterrian had secured the horses before they had entered the thorn covered forest, Zahara and Haneef appear to wilt from relief seeing the five horse's coats glistening from the sunlight shining down upon them; these horses seeming as gifts from heaven to the travelers who had scaled mountains and crossed the desert on foot during their journey and escape.

Chapter 14

The four weary travelers mount and turn their horses north east heading towards the kingdom of Celesador, the three who were questing and the once lost prince. Each of them riding on top a regal steed, with Willetic's leading the rider less horse through the Sandanzo trees without restraint. The price and his childhood playmate frolic amongst the large tree trunks, racing their borrowed horses. Joy circulating through their veins at the fulfilment of the quest they had completed. The weight of finding the price lifted from all of their shoulders, and the excitement of returning him to his rightful place, at the sides of those who have missed him the most, apparent in the easy banter now established between all four of them.

As the sun begins to lower over the four horsemen riding quickly through the trees, Caterrian says, voice carrying to the spread out group, "Let us stop and eat before we reach our final destination."

Bowing her head slightly Zahara responds, "We have no food left."

Willetic chuckles and says to Haneef, "Check in the satchel attached to your saddle."

Clumsily the young prince turns in his saddle, still riding the horse and feels for the satchel on his horse's side. "Oh bread, and salted saniff as well." Haneef says with boyish excitement, "There is a clearing just ahead, we can pause there for our dinner?"

"That looks like a great place to stop and rest our horses and eat before we finish our ride." Caterrian responds through a smile, looking at Willetic who was smiling at the young prince's excitement as well.

They each dismount once the clearing is reached, and untie the satchel from each saddle. Zahara, who had been rationing her food since she had left her father's meadow and Haneef, whose food have been rationed for him the past nine years, quickly dug into the food supply that had attached to their horses. None of the travelers spoke while they ate their fill, each one excited to reach the prince's home.

Looking to the long lost heir, Caterrian says, thinking out loud, "The will have many questions for you once you return home."

Willetic snorts, "I have questions of my own."

Haneef slows in his devouring the bread he is holding, and looks up to the two men who had helped assist in his flight from his former prison. "Why would they question me?" He asks, confusion showing on his naïve face. He looks to Zahara and says, "you know as much as I do."

"But we are not the royal heir." Zahara tells him quietly.

Willetic adds, "We know the parts during which we journeyed to reach you and what occurred while we traveled with you, but this is your story to be told."

Caterrian says quietly, "Your parents will want to hear the account from you, and not from another, only then will their fears be resolved."

"How far are we from the castle?" Zahara asks of the rouge solider.

Caterrian looks at the surrounding and as the position of the sun. "We can reach the castle just after night falls."

"After nightfall?" The Prince asks warily.

"If we ride quick and steady we will be seated with your family by midnight." Caterrian triumphantly tells the prince.

Willetic sees the hesitation and anxiety written on the prince's face. "Caterrian, we have traveled far today, isn't there an inn where we can rest the night?"

"An inn, why would we stop tonight, we have just a short distance left to go?" Caterrian questions his companions.

Zahara looks from Haneef to Willetic and sees the same clues that Willetic had picked up on, she stretches the full to her full ability, over exaggerating an exhaustion that was not present, going as far as to feign a yawn as well. "I agree with Willetic, a good night's sleep in a proper bed would be appreciated." She smiles a serene smile to Haneef.

A confused Caterrian looks at his three traveling companions who moments before seemed as excited as he. He shakes his head still befuddled by the abrupt change in his friends, "Well shall we continue on to Mount Celeste there is an inn in the village that lies at the foot of the mountain, just before we reach the lands outside the walls of Castle Corundum."

Haneef, pacified that he has one final night before his triumphant return to his family once again is buoyant as he gathers the items that had been secured to his borrowed horse, says to his friends and rescuers, "Let us race to the inn, maybe we can reach it before nightfall." The found prince leaps onto the back of his horse and laughing at his exuberant nature, the other three follow his lead, mounting their horses and canter off behind him as they head towards Haneef's mountain.

Chapter 15

The four returning adventures continue their journey through the salahzo trees but with each stride of his horse, Willetic loses his careless banter as he begins to watch the surrounding area instead of just the path before him, knowing that the Picghana tribe sends scouts through the woods to ensure none of the Macindosa tribe can be found close to their village. And as the chieftain his capture would bring great honor to the scouts.

Caterrian notices the change in the air around the agile chieftain and he remembers how they had met, "Willetic are you beginning to fear your old foes?"

Feeling more at ease with the knowledge that Caterrian was also mindful of their surroundings and the possible dangers of the course they were taking to reach their destination in such a quick manner. Willetic snorts with laughter "No fear; just a watchful eye."

Suddenly the path before them was blocked by Picghanan scouts. Haneef still leading them is the first of the four to see the silent scouts standing in their way, he sees them at the same time as his horse, which rears up and unseats the prince, sending him to the ground with a thump.

Seeing the startled prince land on his backside in the dirt, Zahara pulls her own horse's reins shouting "whoa" bringing her horse to stop just feet away from Haneef. Zahara's quick stop jars Caterrian and Willetic from their conversation and they both stop their horses, seeing the Picghana scouts and the downed prince.

"Get down from your horses, you ride with the Macindosan Chief, and so you are now all our prisoners." The Picghanan who was leading the scouts calls out to the three riders who had stalled their horses.

Zahara paying no mind to the weapons that each tribesman held in their caramel colored hands dismounts her horse, dropping the reins to the ground in her dash to Haneef's side. "Are you hurt, Haneef are you alright?" She reaches out her hands towards him, thinking only to search for possible broken bones as the prince had yet to open his eyes from his fall.

"Zahara, there is nothing wrong with me, aside from a bruised backside, and dented ego," Haneef says, opening his eyes and pushing himself up to a seated position in the middle of the path before he looks to his horse, now being calmed by one of the scouts who had scared him to unseat his rider.

"There are too many for me to best this time rouge," Willetic quietly says to Caterrian as they both alight from their horses.

"There are four swords among us this time." Caterrian replies quickly, hopeful that it would be enough to ensure their escape.

"They have already sent news back to the village, more Picghana" he spat as he spoke their name, "warriors are already heading towards us." Willetic sighs fearing that it is his fault that their quest will end before they are able to return the prince to his family.

The rouge and the Chief walk to where Zahara and Haneef still sit on the dirt of the path, Willetic stretches out his hand to assist Haneef to his feet as Caterrian places both his hands under Zahara's underarms and hauls her to her feet and positioning her behind him.

"I am sorry prince that my foes will hold up the return that we have planned for you," Willetic bows his head to Haneef releasing his hand.

Upon hearing the Macindosan Chieftain humbling himself to this child, the Picghana scout leader Tellar looks to his tribesman in question before he says to them, "Gather their horses, Chief Teremun will reward us greatly for them as well as for bringing in this vermin." His fellow scouts hurry and collect the now loose horses as he and two others disarm the four journey weary adventurers and secure their hands with ropes before they lead the pilfered horses and the captured travelers off the path and toward the Picghana village.

"Why do they have quarrel with you?" Haneef asks Willetic, not knowing of the war between the tribes since his capture so many years ago.

Caterrian and Willetic share a glance between themselves before Willetic responds, "Young prince, to these men I am very valuable."

"Valuable, how are you more valuable than I?" Haneef questions him, "who would be of more value than the heir to Cleseador?"

Caterrian notices that the Picghana tribesmen are listening closely to the conversation between the Chieftain and this boy and begins to make small movements in attempts to free his hands from the bonds that hold him.

"Haneef, no one knows of your return, no one knows that you have been found." Zahara says very quietly to the young royal. "I told no one that I was even going out in search, and I know that my father would have never thought that I would find you so quickly."

"While I did tell my superior that I would not give up on my quest to find you, without the men that he sent coming back to him with news that you have been found, no one will have been told that you would be returning." Caterrian adds stilling his movements once he joins in on the conversation.

Now that the Picghanan scouts have listened to the Chief of their enemies and his companions during the length of the trip from the capture to the edge of their village, they begin to murmur amongst themselves.

"Prince Haneef, but isn't he dead."

"They are trying to trick us."

"Could it be true? Is this the long lost heir?"

Tellar, unsure of what course should be taken, says to the scouts, "Teremun will find the truth from the filth once he brings him to trial." This one statement silencing not only the Picghana scouts but the prince, the peasant warrior, the rouge and the Chieftian all fell silent in the knowledge that their fate now lies in the hands of the Picghana Chief.

Chapter 16

The Picghana scouts lead their hostages through the tree line and into the outskirts of their village, marching them past the row of huts that ring the outer edge of the village, Tellar sends one scout to alert their chief of their return. Chief Teremun meets them at the center of the village, smiling when he sees Willetic being led through his village with his people standing watching the once mighty chief lowered to his prisoner bound in restraints.

"Welcome to the Picghana village." Chief Teremun says, his arms outstretched, "I hope you will enjoy the accommodations we have set for you."

Tellar scurries to the chief's side, eager to tell him of the conversation that he had overheard.

"Who? Which one?" Teremun's crashing voice shook the branches of the trees.

The scout slowly nods his head toward the still filthy child whose appearance lacked any royal bearings.

Haneef looks up and he meets the hard stare of Chief Teremun of the Picghana tribe, though he wanted nothing more than to hide behind anyone who would stand between them, the young Prince straightens his shoulders and smiles to his newest captor, hiding his fear behind the royalty he had not used, or remembered for nine years.

"Bring the chief to my hut. The others leave them bound here until I have made a decision as to their fate." Teremun turns and stalks back the way he had entered the village center. He swats at the door to his home slamming it open before entering and taking a seat before the hearth.

Tellar leads Willetic into the chief's home by the ropes that still bind his hands; he pushes the prisoner to the center of the hut. "Your prisoner Chief Teremun," Tellar says haughtily before he exits the hut closing the door behind him.

Willetic raises his bound hands and his eyebrows at the same time, wordlessly asking for the respect of one chieftain to another. Teremun nods and gestures Willetic to him, he takes out a dagger and cuts the ties that held his hands.

"Explain to me what my scout has told me." Teremun says as he waves Willetic to a chair.

"What your scout has told you is the truth," Willetic confirms for Teremun. "The girl found the prince in the Castle of Shade and rescued him. We found them in the Swap of Sorrows, rescued them from a petilo serpent. Caterrian, the rouge and I have journeyed with them to ensure the safe return of the prince to his father, King Mosyan."

"You have found him? You found the heir of Celesador?" Teremun sat back in his chair struck by the news of who his scouts had captured.

"The boy has been kept the past nine years by Queen Mallari's sisters, locked in a cell, bound by chains. Tonight we journey to Castello, the village on the base of Mount Celeste, so that the young Prince can rest there before being reunited with his family."

It took but a moment for the Picghana chieftain to process the story Willetic had told to him. "Tellar" the chieftain's deafening yell shakes the door of the hut as he summons the scout to his hut once more.

"Chieftain" Tellar says as he enters the hut.

"Release the prisoners immediately." Teremun says to the scout.

"Release sir?" the scout asks, looking from Chief Teremun to the man that he had captured who now sat before a fire with his arms draped over the back of the chair in which he sat.

"Yes Tellar, release them and bring them to me." Teremun nods his head.

The scout, expecting praise and honor, walks slowly to the village center, and before the villagers who still stood waiting for the Chief to declare their fate, Tellar cuts the ropes from Zahara and Haneef, and as he turns to cut the ties from Caterrian, the rouge shakes his wrists and the rope falls to the ground between them.

Caterrian smirks at the scout, "I was merely attempting to find more comfort during my stay here in your village."

"Follow me," Tellar grumbles to the three outsiders, feeling the questioning eyes of his people upon him. As he leads them from the meeting place he begins to hear their mutterings.

"Why have they been untied?"

"Where is he taking them?"

Once he reaches the door of Teremun's hut he turns to them and says, "I do not know why my honorable capture of the Macindosan chief has been revoked but my chief has granted your release and has asked for you to be brought before him privately." The disgruntled scout pushes open the door and motions them into the hut.

As Caterrian, Zahara and Haneef enter the Picghanan chieftain's hut, both of the chieftains rise from their seats. Teremun turns to look to Willetic for one last validation of the information that this boy is truly the long lost prince, the heir to Celesador, but Willetic no longer stands, he was once more kneeling before Prince Haneef. When Caterrian and Zahara see that Willetic is once more humbling himself before the prince, they turn and kneel before the royal heir, leaving the Picghana chief the only one still standing in the presence of Prince Haneef.

Teremun kneels, "Prince Haneef, we did not know that you were alive. You have my deepest apologies that you were bound by my men. I pledge my men to your service. Tonight, they will provide you safe passage to where you are going."

Haneef looks from Teremun to Willetic, "Willetic, we are free to go?"

Willetic stands, laughing at the young royal's question, "Yes young sir, as you predicted, you have much more value than a lowly Chieftain such as I."

Caterrian also stands and leans against the frame of the door, arms crossed in front of him, "Well Willetic, I could have told you that you have inflated the value you hold anywhere but in your own mind."

Willetic walks towards Caterrian, but steps next to the prince first, he leans close to Haneef and whispers under his breath, "I bowed once to prove my loyalty," with a smile he continues, "this time was to provide his."

Haneef laughs at the natural banter of his friends and traveling companions, not noticing that Zahara took longer than the rest in rising to her feet and her lean against the wall was more of a slump to Caterrian's haughty stance.

Chapter 17

The five horses once more freshly groomed and fed are led to the place where Haneef, Zahara, Caterrian and Chief Willetic stand with satchels of fresh food for each of them. As they prepare for the final leg of their journey for the night, Zahara watches as the sun continues to set to the west over the evil lands through which they had toiled. But Willetic still alert unsure if he fully trusts the Picghana scout who had captured them just hours before instead is keeping an eye on the tribesman who are gathering weapons and readying horses. Caterrian and Haneef both mount their horses and turn their horses in the direction of Mount Celeste.

Teremun walks up to the eight scouts that are preparing to guard the prince during this final stage of his journey home, "Tellar, ride ahead with Willetic and ensure that there are no scouting parties out who may try and stop the prince. If you ride together"

Willetic nods as he walks up to the chief, "Either tribe will know we have safe passage."

Teremun slaps Willetic on the back, a gesture that would send most men stumbling, but Willetic stands firm, "Exactly."

The scout nods his head to show that he understands the directive that his Chieftain has provided, "As you say chieftain." Tellar turns and mounts his horse.

The other seven scouts follow his lead and mount their horses, bringing their horses to circle the prince's entourage as the sun finishes setting and the stars shine bright in the sky.

One of the scouts reins his horse next to Zahara who has yet to climb onto her horse. "Girl, do you need help? I can see that you are fatigued."

Haneef sees the Picghanan scout talking to Zahara and he turns his horse towards her, until he observes that she spurns his offer and pulls herself onto her saddle and she begins to lead them on towards Castello.

Willetic and Tellar prompt their horses ahead of the group to survey the route the Prince will travel. As soon as they cross out of the village, Tellar spurs his horse, bringing his horse in front of the chieftain. "Keep up chief," the Picghanan spat, "We have to gain distance to protect this Prince."

Willetic leans forward, urging his horse faster, but keeps the scout in front him, allowing him to perceive that he is leading so that the chief can keep a careful eye on this Picghanan spy.

Riding at a much slower pace Zahara leads the royal entourage along with the Picghanans through the woods towards the inn where she will finally have the chance to rest.

Tellar and Willetic reach the inn and they both dismount. Willetic leaves his horse with the stable master and turns to go in to secure chambers for the group that will be arriving soon, while Tellar leads his horse around towards the back of the inn with Willetic watching him turn the corner and disappear behind the building under guarded eyes before entering the front door of the establishment.

"Innkeep, I need four rooms for the night," the Macindosan chieftain says as he reaches the bar.

"Ah chief, let me make the arraignments for you." The Castelloian inn owner greets him. "Chambermaid, free up four rooms for this worthy noble."

The maid sets down the tray she was carrying and dips her head before she goes into the kitchen and up to the second floor.

Willetic sits at the corner of the bar to wait for Caterrian, Zahara and the Prince, ignoring the mug the innkeeper sets before him, keeping a watchful eye on the door unsure if Tellar plans to come inside or if he is waiting out in the dark night.

The prince and the group leading him home reach the inn. While Caterrian gathers the horses and bring them into the stable the Picghana tribesman alight from their horses and stand outside the stable watching the royal youth as he and Zahara enter the hostel.

"Will you return to your village tonight?" Catterian inquires of the scouts who helped safeguard Prince Haneef in their star lit trek.

"We will wait out the sun rise here," the tallest of the Picghana scouts says to the Rouge.

Caterrian nods, "I will have warm bread sent out to you." And the rouge sets back his shoulders, knowing that he must once more take on the colors of the king's guards, he shakes out the cloak that had ridden with him in a satchel on his horse, bearing the king's emblem and he shrugs it over his strapping shoulders before he enters the inn to find his newly found companions.

Willetic, Zahara and Haneef sit at the bar with four bowls of stew set before them. The prince and the peasant warrior have already begun to gobble down the warm food in front of them, while Willetic still sits back; watching for the rouge to come inside, but instead of the rouge soldier, Caterrian the third in command of the king's guard enters through the front doors. The chieftain smiles seeing the change in Caterrian's demeanor, as Caterrian is stopped over and over by the different towns people wishing him well and welcoming him home from the quest, little did they know that sitting in the room with them was the prince that had been lost to the kingdom of Celesador.

Seeing the two Celesadorians youth eating with so much gusto, Caterrian motions to Willetic to join him as he sits a an empty table just out of hearing of the bar where Zahara and Haneef sit. Willetic picks up the two cooling bowls of stew and signals to the owner of the establishment for mugs of mulled berries to be brought to their table and goes to sit with Caterrian.

"Tomorrow will be here before too long." Caterrian says by way of greeting.

"Are you ready for your triumphant return," Willetic chuckles, setting the bowls on the table.

"Do you think that Haneef is ready to return to royalty?" Caterrian muses stirring his stew while Willetic begins to eat.

The two sit contemplating the upcoming day while they continue to eat their food, when suddenly the sound of laughter is heard coming from the bar. They look over to Haneef and Zahara who are reminiscing of their childhood and laughing at the antics of their fathers.

"They have missed each other." Caterrian muses.

Willetic smiles at the youth's laughter. "They have so much more to say to each other, and they don't even know it," he says to Caterrian. "It takes much more than just courage to search as she did."

"She has something more impelling her choices to put her life up as collateral in this quest as she did." Caterrian agrees with WIlletic. "But he doesn't realize it yet."

"He needs time to re-acclimate to not only society, but to his royal status before he will even be able to notice the connection they have."

Caterrian laughs, "Isn't it nice to know that things have finally come together as they are supposed to."

Just then, Zahara and Haneef stand and walk up to their table.

"I am going to head up to a room; I can hear the bed calling out to me." Haneef says attempting to hide a yawn.

Zahara looks candidly around the main room of the inn's downstairs, seeing the lack of females excluding the serving maids, "I too am going to up to my room" she says with a soft smile.

The two seated laugh at her candid way of stating that she had noticed that the clientele has changed to a less than savory crowd. Caterrian nods to them as WIlletic once more signals to the innkeeper.

"The chambermaid will show you both to your rooms," the chieftain says to them.

The two youth nod to their friends as they turn and follow the maid up to the second floor. They pass an room with an open door before stopping at the second room, the maid pushes the door fully open and steps back, "Miss this is the room we have prepared for you," the young servant girl shows her the basin of warm water setting near to the fire lit in the small hearth.

"Good night Zahara, I will see you come morning." Haneef says as the maid continues to the next room down the hall.

Zahara stands watching him until he enters his room. "Sleep well Haneef." She whispers as he closes the door behind him before she closes her own door and walks up to the basin of water. Even though she is exhausted enough to ignore any grooming in favor of lying down on the soft bed in the corner of the small room, Zahara removes her hooded cloak and tunic. She sees the tear in the left sleeve of her tunic, and turns to look into the small mirror on the wall near the door. The scratch that was left on her left arm by the sting of the petilo's tail red in color and streaks can be seen from the poison that is beginning to spread through her blood. The young girl slowly turns back to the water bowl and gently begins to wash her battle wound.

Chapter 18

Caterrian and Willetic finish their bowls of stew and sit talking while sipping on the mugs the innkeeper had brought to them.

"I am going to go and check that our horses have been brushed and given plenty of feed before I turn in for the remainder of the night." Willetic pushes his empty cup to the middle of the wooden table.

Caterrian stops the Macindosan by raising his hand before he is able to fully excuse himself from the table, "I promised our Picghanan friends some warm bread as they plan to stand guard for us tonight, if you will please take it out to them." He pauses to drain the last of the mulled berries from his mug, "I will be turning in as well as soon as I finish my mug of mead."

"Your glass is empty though," Willetic points to the mug that had just been emptied.

"This glass is, but I plan to drink mead until I am drunk tonight, so I have many more glasses left to drink." Caterrian says with a mischievous grin.

Willetic grabs the basket of bread, shaking his head as he walks out to distribute the food to the tribesmen who are standing guard through the dark night. Assuming that they will be positioned just beyond the courtyard, Willetic calls out, "I have the bread that was promised to you."

"It is a good thing you made your self known Macindosan," one of the scouts says with a quick laugh as he steps out from the tree cover, "you were our captive earlier today." He takes the basket from Willetic, "Thank you, I will make sure everyone gets their fill," before he disappears once more into the trees.

Smiling at the Picghanan scout's banter, Willetic turns and enters the stable to check on the five horses that had been left there.

"Do you need your horse prepared for you sir?" a stable boy steps out of the shadows.

"No boy, I just wanted to check on him, and the four horses that came in together as well." Willetic assures the young boy.

"They are all back here," the lad shows Willetic to the back of the stable where the horses are finishing buckets of grain in their stalls. "I groomed each one myself before filling the buckets of grain for them," the boy says, taking pride in his position at the stable.

"Thank you for looking after them so well," Willetic reaches out his arm, shaking the boys hand as he would the stable master.

The chieftain turns and walks back into the inn, smiling to Caterrian who raises his mug in salute as Willetic walks through the dining hall and goes straight up the stairs to where his bed chamber lies. Leaving the first room open for Caterrian who will still be a while downstairs, Willetic passes the room where Zahara is finishing wrapping a clean rag around the scratch left by the petilo serpent, and then the room where Haneef is finishing washing the dirt from his hair, showing the blond curls that had been hidden for so long, before he reaches the room left open for him. Opening the door, Willetic pauses, looking back over his shoulder before going into the room and laying down to rest his head.

Downstairs Caterrian raises his mug of mead that one of the villagers had purchased for him.

"To our returning hero" the shout can be heard by the Pichganas standing guard outside the inn.

"Here, Here." The entire crowd raises their glasses to the member of the king's guard.

Caterrian smiles as another mug is placed before him, "Imagine how they would cheer if they knew who the boy truly is." He says into his glass before emptying the mug in his hand and slamming it on the table and picking up the fresh mug.

Having drunk every mug that the villagers set before him, Caterrian looks around him at the nearly empty room. The only other occupants left, the serving maid and a few men who could not afford a room, and so they lay their heads on the tables before them. The rouge guard pushes himself back from the table and still steady on his feet, he makes his way up to the room that was left open for him, throws himself on the still made bed, and pulls his cloak around him as he closes his eyes in a deep slumber.

Hearing the quiet in the room next to her, Zahara walks to the door pausing just a moment before she pulls the door open and looks out towards the stairs that lead to the dining hall. She steps out of the room, her normally sure steps falter as she turns away from the stairs and walks down the hall, stopping in front of Haneef's door. The peasant girl stands steps from his door for a few moments before she reaches out her right hand, steps forward and lightly places her hand on the handle. Looking at the door as though she can see straight through it, Zahara leans in to the door, touching the center of the door with her left hand at the same moment she rests her forehead against it. She takes a deep yet shaky breath in holding the air in her lungs she releases the door knob and brings her right hand to grasp the bandaged scratch on her left arm. As she exhales, Zahara pushes off the door, turns to the left, letting her back gently hit the wall that separates her and the prince, and she finally allows herself to wilt as the severity of the small cut, the only wound she received throughout her quest to find Haneef, is able to settle in her mind. Now that Haneef is safe she knows that her life will be cut short, just as her best friend has been brought home. With this thought the tears that she has fought since the strike of the tail landed on her arm finally began to fall.

The prince not knowing that Zahara was sitting in the hall outside of his room crying stands at the window in his room. Just as Zahara has a heavy burden that she has been carrying the journey home, Haneef feels the heavy weight of who he is, and what he will be returning to once the sun rises and they reach Castle Corundum and his parents, the king and queen. Looking out the window, his scrutiny fixated on the castle that is his home, the young royal doesn't see the man standing deep in the shadows of the night menacingly looking up at him framed in the window, his blond curls shimmering from the moon light that is shining down upon him. Nor does he see the single black bird that flies west in the ink black sky.

Printed in the United States
By Bookmasters